SHERLOCK HOLMES &
THE SECRET MISSION

It is the spring of 1912 and Dr Watson has decided to retire from practice. In order to rekindle his old friendship with Sherlock Holmes, Watson travels to Sussex for a short holiday. Within hours of his arrival he finds himself drawn into a series of terrible events surrounding the apparent death of Holmes' brother, Mycroft, the mysterious kidnapping of a London safe-maker and a murderous attack upon a seaman. All these events are interrelated and Sherlock Holmes has to discover what lies at the root of it all, be it in London or Rome.

Sherlock Holmes & The Secret Mission

by

Eddie Maguire

Dales Large Print Books
Long Preston, North Yorkshire,
BD23 4ND, England.

British Library Cataloguing in Publication Data.

Maguire, Eddie
    Sherlock Holmes & the secret mission.

    A catalogue record of this book is
    available from the British Library

    ISBN   978-1-84262-565-1 pbk

First published in Great Britain in 2005
under the Breese Books Imprint
by the Irregular Special Press for Baker Street Studios Ltd.

Published in Large Print 2007 by arrangement with
Baker Street Studios Ltd.

Dales Large Print is an imprint of Library Magna Books Ltd.

Printed and bound in Great Britain by
T.J. (International) Ltd., Cornwall, PL28 8RW

ONE

The winter of 1911/12 had been a harsh one. Although little snow had fallen, the cold and damp conditions had made my life little short of intolerable. I suppose it must have been a combination of the Jezail bullet collected in Afghanistan, so many years ago, and the ageing process which caused me to suffer much discomfort.

My practice, for so many years a constant source of interest and satisfaction, had recently become a chore. Too often, I found myself in consultation with a patient who appeared to be in far better health than myself. Their coughs, colds, pains and their petty complaints were more than I could endure. I therefore came to a decision; I would retire from practice. Jacks, my young assistant, was a more than adequate replacement. Moreover, he still retained his youthful enthusiasm, which by now was so lacking in myself.

It was on the first of March 1912, that I made this momentous decision as I returned to my quarters at 221B Baker Street and considered what the future would hold for me. The rooms, which I had shared for so many years with Sherlock Holmes, could hardly be described as a home. There were reminders of Holmes, but Holmes himself was gone to Sussex.

Mrs Hudson, for so long our landlady, had retired the previous year and the property had come into the hands of a 'friendly society'. The company installed a Mrs Blair, as a caretaker rather than as a housekeeper. On that matter, Mrs Blair had quickly put me right. 'I don't do no cooking, Doctor Watson, so you'll have to have your meals out. I don't do no washing neither, so you'll have to make your own arrangements. My son George will bring you the coal, but you'll have to make up your own fire and I clean through on Wednesdays, so I expect you'll be about your business that day.'

She also had a strong objection to 'being put upon'. It was never exactly explained what Mrs Blair meant by this, but I assumed that it was any labour, which interfered with her indolent lifestyle.

I threw my keys onto the table and attacked the fire with the poker. Before long I had a merry blaze going. I drew some water from the tap in the dressing room and filled the little black kettle, which I placed on the fire stand.

Later, as I settled down with my *Telegraph*, an idea came creeping into my mind. How long had it been since I had seen my old friend Sherlock Holmes? Six months? I would telegraph him directly and ask him to come and visit me.

The reply came the very next morning. It read:

CLIFF HOUSE – FULWORTH – SUSSEX
MY DEAR WATSON
HOW SPLENDID TO HEAR FROM YOU AGAIN – I AM PRESENTLY UN-ABLE TO LEAVE MY EXPERIMENTS – I DO SUGGEST, HOWEVER, THAT YOU COME DOWN TO SUSSEX – I WILL EXPECT TO HEAR FROM YOU IN THE AFFIRMATIVE.
HOLMES

I chuckled as I read the telegram. How exactly like Holmes. He had retired from the fray, but was clearly unable to vegetate quietly. No doubt he was hard at work investigating the properties of some substance or other. Accordingly I telegraphed back that I would see him at the weekend.

The morning of my journey to Sussex dawned crisp and bright. As I boarded the train to Newhaven, my mind still harboured worries about my reception, then it occurred to me that I was crossing my bridges before I came to them. I therefore resolved to let nature take its course and, turning to the Telegraph crossword, I promptly forgot my troubles.

The train pulled into Newhaven station. Standing on the platform was the angular figure I knew so well.

'Watson, my dear fellow.'

'Holmes, it is good to see you again.'

Sherlock Holmes picked up my gladstone. 'Come along, Doctor, I have a carriage waiting in the lane.'

Very soon we were bowling along the lanes of Sussex. The air seemed somehow clearer and fresher than in London. Holmes turned and smiled. 'A capital day, is it not?' He gestured towards the road before us. 'I often think that, in winter, we see the real world. The bare bones where nothing is masked by finery and frippery.'

I laughed. 'Why, you have almost become poetic.'

The next few days passed swiftly. Holmes and I tramped over the rolling downs which surrounded his villa. Each morning we would set out, keen to explore whilst the weather held, and each afternoon we would return, cold and hungry, to enjoy a well-deserved supper prepared by the excellent Mrs Oliver, the housekeeper.

It was over such a supper, three days after my arrival, when Holmes mentioned the subject of his brother.

'Mycroft,' I said. 'Is he still at the heart of all things important to England's affairs?'

Holmes sighed. 'Indeed, Doctor. It is unfortunate that my brother has become all too indispensable. Often has he written to me of his intention to fade into oblivion, but there is always another crisis just around the corner and it is to Mycroft the Ministers always turn.'

'How fortunate are we, that we can take the decision to retire when the time suits us.'

Holmes pushed back his chair and moved to the old leather sofa before the fire. 'Ah, but you have not heard the best of it, Watson. As you are perfectly well aware, my brother's activities revolve around his club and his office. Yet, by some miracle, the Foreign Office has managed to separate him from his usual haunts. He is presently on his way back from Rome.'

'Good heavens!' I cried. 'The matter must indeed be of a serious nature.'

There was a knock at the door and Mrs Oliver appeared. 'Your coffee, gentlemen.'

'Thank you, Mrs Oliver,' said Holmes.

'If there's nothing else, Mr Holmes, I'll be off. It is almost dark and it's a fair step to Fulworth.'

I poured the coffee and handed a cup to Holmes. 'Now then, what has occurred that is important enough to knock Mycroft off his rails?'

Holmes sipped at his coffee. 'As you know, Watson, I take little interest in matters of state. I did learn that it was an affair of the utmost importance and it was something to do with one of the crowned heads of Europe.'

'Hmm, that is not very illuminating. There is talk of sedition in several of Europe's great states. The news-papers these days speak of little else.'

'Yes, but it must be something more, Watson. Something out of the ordinary, an occurrence which is new and unique.'

'Ah well, in a few days, Mycroft will have returned and we will know the truth.'

Sherlock Holmes and I sat talking well

10

into the night, but at last, wearied by the late hour, I said goodnight and made my way to my bed. I was asleep almost as soon as my head touched the pillow.

Suddenly, I was awake once more. It was still quite dark and the stars were glittering in the frosty sky. I reached for my vestas and struck one. In the light of the flame, I could see that it was almost five o'clock. For a moment, I was unsure what it was that had so abruptly awakened me. Then, I became aware of voices. Three, perhaps four, people were talking excitedly.

I slipped out of bed and pulled on my dressing gown. My service revolver, so often a companion on dark and dangerous nights, I slipped into the pocket. I turned the knob and opened the door a little. The voices were coming from upstairs in Holmes's book-lined garret.

Then the door opened and flooded the stair in light. It was Holmes, his face as white as chalk. I ran up the short flight, concerned for my friend. 'Holmes, what on earth is the matter?' I cried.

'Watson, my dear fellow. I was about to wake you. We have visitors. Visitors who bring grave news.'

Holmes led me into the presence of his

guests. They were two men I knew well, Sir Arthur Richardson, first Secretary to the Cabinet Office and General James Wilton, Military Adviser to the Prime Minister. Sir Arthur had been a regular visitor to 221B Baker Street some years before when he had been plain Arthur Richardson, a young Civil Servant in his first posting. The general I knew as a brother officer in Afghanistan, more years ago than I care to remember.

There was no fire and the room was cold, but colder still was the attitude of Sherlock Holmes. 'Watson, these gentlemen have brought me news of Mycroft. He is ill and in a sanatorium close by to Rome.' He turned and frowned at our guests. 'Apparently the trip was too much for him. His health of late has been poor and yet they asked him to go to Italy, instead of sending a younger, fitter, man.'

'Good heavens, is this true?'

Sir Arthur looked at his feet for a moment before speaking. 'Yes, Doctor Watson, I am sorry to say that Mr Holmes is speaking the truth. But you must understand, sir. The matter was of European importance and Mr Mycroft Holmes was the only man in whom we could place our complete trust and reliance.'

'But surely there was someone else,' I said. 'Mycroft is his brother's senior by seven years. It is too much to ask a man of his years to undertake a secret mission.'

Sir Arthur cast a worried glance at Holmes before answering. When he spoke, it was as if he had made up his mind. 'The mission was of such importance that no one else could be entrusted with it. So serious was the matter that a less acute mind than that of Mr Holmes could not have been sent. The matter of the life of the Tsar of Russia could not be handled by a lesser man.'

General Wilton stiffened and uttered a muted oath, but he was waved aside by Sir Arthur. 'Mr Holmes has a right to know, James. I must tell him in order to make him understand.'

Sir Arthur sat opposite Holmes at the table and spread his hands out before him. 'Mr Holmes, some six weeks ago we received word from one of our agents that the Tsar of Russia had become ill. He had suffered sick headaches and aching limbs; a general lethargy had overcome him. The Tsarina had suffered likewise. At first, it was feared that cholera might be the cause, but medical tests proved negative. He continues to be unwell, but his doctors cannot

13

discover why.

'Last week the same agent reported that a strong rumour has gone around St Petersburg that the Tsar and Tsarina are being poisoned and that someone from the Royal Family is implicated.'

Sherlock Holmes moved from his chair and pulled back the curtain a little. The first faint glow of morning was lighting the sky. 'The fact that someone should wish the Tsar dead is not a surprise, Sir Arthur. For too long he has let matters slip. People are starving in Russia, yet he does nothing to alleviate their condition.'

'But good heavens, Holmes,' I said. 'A member of his own family...'

'Indeed, but perhaps it is someone who desires to see an end to all tsars. Why not one of his own family?'

'Mr Holmes may be correct, Doctor Watson,' said Sir Arthur. 'Ever since 1905 there has been serious unrest in Russia.'

During the conversation Holmes had managed to get a fire going. His task completed, he turned to Sir Arthur with a look that brooked no dissent. 'Was the safety of the Tsar the only reason my brother was sent to Rome?'

Sir Arthur quailed under the steely gaze of

Sherlock Holmes. 'No, Mr Holmes. The Balkan situation was also to be discussed. Serbia in particular is proving to be particularly aggressive towards Austria and is actively encouraging Slovenia and Croatia, whom she believes to be rightly within her sphere of influence, to rebel against their Austrian masters and form a south Slav republic.

'Vital to her aims is the special relationship that Serbia enjoys with her Russian neighbour. It is our information that the Tsar would look favourably on any attempt by Serbia to form such an alliance and would facilitate any movement in that direction, perhaps with troops. This would almost certainly lead to a war in Europe. This His Majesty's government cannot allow.'

'Then it is clear to me,' said Holmes, 'that you are prepared to abandon the Tsar to his fate.'

Sir Arthur sighed wearily. 'If it were only as simple as that, Mr Holmes. His Majesty's government has decided that whilst it could support a new Parliamentary regime in Russia, it never would countenance any forcible removal of the Tsar. If he were to be persuaded to abdicate in favour of his brother, Michael, or indeed if he could become a constitutional monarch then politicians all over Europe, including myself, would sleep more easily in their beds at night.'

Sherlock Holmes held a spill to the fire, then lit his pipe. 'It appears, Sir Arthur, that your assertion that my brother was the only man able for the task has been vindicated.'

Sir Arthur said nothing but slightly inclined his head in acknowledgement.

'You remarked earlier that the Foreign Office had been told that Mycroft was ill. Did you receive a letter in his own hand?' asked Holmes.

'No, Mr Holmes, the Foreign Office received a wire in his name stating the facts. Indeed, I believe that the general has a copy on his person.'

General Wilton reached for his top pocket and produced a single folded sheet of paper, which he handed to Sherlock Holmes.

'Now, let me see. It reads:

AM PRESENTLY UNWELL – UNABLE TO ATTEND CONFERENCE – WILL WIRE AGAIN WHEN RECOVERED – DIOGENES.

'His *nom de guerre*, I presume. Well, his illness appears to be trivial. Perhaps he will be well again quite soon.'

I glanced at my watch. 'Good heavens, it is almost seven o'clock. Mrs Oliver will be here quite soon to begin breakfast.'

Breakfast for Sir Arthur and the general was a perfunctory affair. Their driver was expected at seven-thirty so it was a matter of toast and coffee. Holmes and I, however, settled down to what the hoteliers call 'a full English breakfast'.

Sir Arthur took his hat from the stand and held out his hand. 'Goodbye, Mr Holmes. Thank you for being so understanding about your brother. Goodbye, Doctor Watson.'

Holmes and Sir Arthur went out together. General Wilton clapped me on the shoulder. 'Well, goodbye, John. It is a pity that we should meet again under such a cloud.'

Moments later Sherlock Holmes reappeared in the doorway. He rubbed his hands together briskly. 'Well now, Watson. What do you make of that?'

'I must say that I find it a little strange to have important men such as Sir Arthur and General Wilton visit you in the dead of night, then leave again at daybreak.'

Holmes laughed. 'My dear, Watson. On the contrary, I find it wholly consistent with normal secret activities. They had to be seen to leave their desks last night as usual and then return to them again this morning, as if nothing was happening to upset the normal machinations of the Foreign Office. Without such confidences as Sir Arthur revealed his mission would not have succeeded.'

'Mission?' I exclaimed. 'Forgive me, Holmes, but I was not aware that Sir Arthur had more on his mind than the matter of your brother's health.'

Once again Holmes laughed. 'If I may mix my sporting metaphors, Watson. Sir Arthur's task was to get me on side and then prepare me to be a backstop. Indeed, I was somewhat surprised to find that he departed with the question he was sent to ask me, left unasked.'

I felt myself to be all at sea and floundering. 'What on earth do you mean, Holmes?'

Sherlock Holmes perched himself on the edge of the kitchen table and looked carefully at me with those piercing grey eyes of his. 'Well, to get me on side, Watson, Sir Arthur had to explain fully the situation. He had to secure my understanding of the importance of the mission. He needed my tacit approval. Likewise, if it becomes apparent that Mycroft is really unwell, the Foreign Office would be in need of a replacement in whom it can place its complete trust.'

'Of course,' I said, 'exit Mycroft, enter Sherlock.'

'Exactly,' he replied. 'After all, once I had given my approval, I could hardly refuse to assist His Majesty's government if the need arose.'

'Well, Sir Arthur has nicely manoeuvred you into a corner, Holmes.'

Holmes slid gently off the table. 'Then let us sincerely hope that brother Mycroft quickly regains his health.'

The weather that day proved to be extremely unsettled. Holmes and I quickly decided that inaction should be the best course of action. At least, that was my decision. After an early luncheon, I took a book into the study where, before a roaring fire, I alternately read and dozed. Holmes for his part disappeared into his workshop and buried himself in one or other of his innumerable experiments.

It was after three p.m. when I awoke with a start. My book had slipped to the floor. Holmes was standing in front of the fire warming himself, an expression of extreme satisfaction on his face. 'Ah, Watson, my dear fellow. Tea is being served. Mrs Oliver looked in a few moments ago and has asked me to awaken you. She also stated that you looked so sweet sleeping with your book in your hand. It is, however, not an opinion to which I hold. Sleeping when you should be engaged in some more profitable occupation!'

I yawned and stretched. 'If you mean that I should be busy filling the house with similar noxious smells to the ones you have been producing, then I cannot agree.'

'Ah, but there is method in my madness. I believe that I have the clue to the matter of the Romanovs' illness.'

'You have?'

'Indeed.'

'Is it poison?'

'Yes Doctor. It is undoubtedly arsenic. Small doses can be readily introduced into the food and drink without violent reaction. I have perused a medical tome, which I purchased last year, and the Romanovs have all the classic symptoms of arsenic poisoning.'

'Good heavens!'

'Moreover, I have also been able to re-create Doctor Marsh's test for arsenic absorption whilst you were lying there looking sweet. All that I now require is a sample of the Tsar's hair and I can prove my theory.'

I stood up and smiled. 'Well, should you ever be so fortunate as to run into the Tsar, perhaps you can persuade him to let you have a lock of his hair for your experimentation.'

The spell of foul weather had passed and the morning dawned crisp and clear.

At breakfast there was no sign of Holmes. Mrs Oliver informed me that he had gone out some time earlier. Then the kitchen door opened and Holmes appeared. 'Watson, my dear fellow, what a capital morning. Mrs Oliver, if Doctor Watson has not appropriated the provisions, I will have my breakfast now, if you please.'

He threw off his ulster and cap. 'Ah, before I forget, Watson. I ran across the postman just now. Here is a letter for you.'

'For me? Who would be writing to me here?'

Holmes picked up the letter and carelessly scanned it. 'It is a letter from a professional man, a doctor. He is, I should judge to be about seven and thirty. He has reddish-brown hair and he wears gold-framed reading glasses.'

'Jacks!' I cried.

'Just so.'

'But how could you know?'

'Elementary, Doctor. Your own monogram

is on the back of the envelope. Young Jacks has had the financial acumen to continue using your old stationery until it is used up.'

'So it is. I did not observe.'

'Exactly. You have exhibited the single most common fault of humanity. You look but you do not see,' he retorted.

'Well, let us see what the young man is writing to me about,' I said, tearing open the envelope. The letter read thus:

9th March, 1912,
84 Devonshire Street,
W.C.

Dear Doctor Watson,

A little over an hour ago, I was listening to a young woman who has told me a singular story.

Her name is Mrs Agnes Andrews. She informed me that six days ago she was unfortunate enough to witness the brutal kidnapping of her husband, Mr Hunter Andrews, owner of H.B. Andrews, the strong-room and safe manufacturers.

The police have so far been unable to ascertain the whereabouts of the unfortunate man and she is, quite understandably, frantic with worry.

Mrs Andrews is convinced that the police have missed vital clues; and without specialist help, Mr Andrews may never be found.

Apparently, Mrs Andrews, knowing your long and fruitful association with Mr Sherlock Holmes, has twice sought you out at your rooms only to be disappointed by your absence. This morning she ascertained the whereabouts of your practice, but was further distressed to discover that you have recently retired.

Is there any way in which you might assist this lady? You, of course, are not Sherlock Holmes, but something of his aptitude must have rubbed off onto you. Perhaps upon your return you could hear Mrs Andrews out and advise her on the steps that she might take to alleviate her situation.

Yours sincerely

Thomas Jacks, M.D.

'Well now, what do you make of that?' I said.

A peculiar glint had come into the eye of Sherlock Holmes. It was a sign I had observed many times before. 'Most intriguing,' he declared. 'There are many loose ends,

Watson. Ah, it is almost a pity I have retired. The case might have proved stimulating.'

'But what am I to do?' I said. 'As Jacks points out, and quite rightly, I am no Sherlock Holmes. I fear that I cannot help the lady.'

'You will have to see her, Doctor.'

I sighed. 'You are quite right, Holmes. Although it will dash her hopes, I shall tell Mrs Andrews that there is nothing I can do to help her.'

The conversation was interrupted by a knock at the kitchen door. Mrs Oliver appeared a few moments later. 'Mr Holmes, a telegram has been delivered for you.'

Holmes and I exchanged glances. A simultaneous thought had entered our minds. He tore open the envelope. 'Watson,' he said tersely, 'you had better pack your bag. We are returning to London.'

'Is it your brother?'

'It is.'

'Very well. Give me ten minutes.'

I ran upstairs and threw my things into my gladstone. A few minutes later Sherlock Holmes and myself were to be found rapidly striding along the Fulworth Road.

'Your brother,' I said. 'He is much worse?'

'Very much worse, Watson. He is dead.'

TWO

The train journey from Newhaven to London was without doubt the most depressing I have ever made. Sherlock Holmes had never been a convivial travelling companion. Often he would slip into a world of his own, uncommunicative and distant. But on this occasion there was something new. A deep, cold anger, such as I had never before experienced. But however discomforted his travelling companion, how much worse would it be for those on whom his anger would be turned.

At Victoria Station, we were met by Sir Arthur Richardson in person. 'Mr Holmes, you have my deepest sympathies.'

Holmes said nothing, merely maintaining a brisk pace to the entrance where Sir Arthur had a cab waiting.

'We shall be travelling to Downing Street,' said Sir Arthur. 'I have made arrangements for your reception there. Lord Falmouth also desires to speak with you and to pass on his personal condolences.'

'Sympathetic utterances are unnecessary, Sir Arthur,' said Holmes. 'His Lordship would be better engaged in relaying the circumstances in which my brother's death occurred.'

Sir Arthur coloured. 'I dare say that he will be happy to oblige, sir.'

At number ten Downing Street we were quickly shown into the green reception room. Lord Falmouth rose from his chair and strode across the room to greet us. Holmes ignored his proffered hand and sat down by the fire.

I took Lord Falmouth's hand and shook it. 'Good morning, sir. You will forgive Holmes, but he has had a nasty shock.'

'Please, Watson. Do not waste your time in idle chatter,' said Holmes icily. 'I am quite sure that Lord Falmouth has other matters to which he must attend. Now, sir,' said Holmes, looking for the first time deeply into the eyes of the Foreign Secretary. 'Exactly how did my brother come to die?'

Lord Falmouth took from the desk a single sheet of paper and held it out for inspection. It was a telegram. Looking over the shoulder of Sherlock Holmes I read the following.

REGRET TO INFORM YOU – SUDDEN DEATH OF DIOGENES – NEW AR-RANGEMENTS MUST BE MADE – PLEASE ADVISE.
KEEBLE.

Holmes threw the telegram onto the desk. 'But this tells me nothing. Have you no other information?'

'No, Mr Holmes. There is nothing more.'

'Very well,' declared Holmes, standing up. 'I do not propose to take up any more of your time. You will inform me of further developments.'

'Indeed,' said Lord Falmouth, rising also.

'For the present I shall be returning to my old rooms at 221B Baker Street. You may contact me there.'

Once again I shook hands with Lord Falmouth. 'Goodbye, sir,' I murmured.

As I followed Holmes, I was stopped by Sir Arthur. 'His lordship seems a little flustered,' he remarked.

'He has encountered Sherlock Holmes at his most incisive.'

A hint of a smile was playing around the official's mouth. He seemed to be amused. 'I do not think that anyone has dared speak like that to his lordship since he was a boy.'

Later, at 221B Baker Street, Mrs Blair was rudely shaken out of her lethargy. So, too, was George, her son. Within the hour, fresh linen had been obtained and the beds made up. A good fire was crackling in the grate and several buckets of coal were in attendance. George was sent out for provisions and Mrs Blair was soon to be heard puffing up the stairs with a tray of tea and sandwiches.

There was a tread on the stairs. The door opened and there stood the figure of an old friend.

'Why, Inspector Lestrade,' said Holmes, jumping up.

'Mr Holmes, Doctor Watson. It is a pleasure to see you again. But, I have to tell you, gentlemen, that you are addressing *Chief* Inspector Lestrade.'

'My dear fellow,' I cried. 'A well-deserved promotion.'

'Thank you, sir.'

'Now, Lestrade, you will take some tea with us,' said Holmes. 'Then perhaps you will inform us of the nature of your visit.'

The detective laid his coat on an upright chair and sat by the fire. 'You see through me, Mr Holmes. Although the pleasure from meeting you both again is indeed grand, my main reason for coming here today is to ask

28

you, Doctor Watson, if you feel able to assist me in a particularly puzzling case. But as I find you here too, Mr Holmes, perhaps you would care to hear me out?'

I could almost feel Holmes's body stiffening.

'Lestrade, you know that Mr Holmes has retired,' I said. 'Moreover, he has today suffered a deep personal loss.'

Sherlock Holmes raised his hand. 'Wait, Watson. Perhaps Lestrade's problem may provide some therapeutic relief. Please continue, Chief Inspector.'

'If you are sure, Mr Holmes,' said the policeman.

'Quite sure.'

'Very well. Some seven days ago a young man was kidnapped almost from outside his own front door. He was assaulted by two muscular men, then bundled into a cab. His wife witnessed the whole thing and she is, not surprisingly, greatly upset.'

'Of course there has been no ransom demand,' said Holmes.

'Good heavens, Mr Holmes!' ejaculated the detective. 'How could you know that?'

'If there had been a ransom demand then, my dear Lestrade, you would hardly have been referring to the kidnapping as particularly puzzling,' said Holmes smoothly.

Lestrade laughed. 'Of course, Mr Holmes. Why, just for a moment I thought you had done something clever there.'

Holmes shot me an expressive glance. 'Very well, Lestrade, let me truly amaze you. The missing man is Mr Hunter Andrews. He is a master carpenter and locksmith.'

The detective sat bolt upright in his chair and spluttered into his tea. Again, Holmes cast a glance in my direction. 'As for the motive, Lestrade, let me suggest to you that Mr Andrews was kidnapped in order to execute a particular task for these gentlemen.'

'Yes,' replied Lestrade eagerly. 'Perhaps you are right. I shall speak with my underworld contacts and discover if there is a particularly big job being planned.' He stood up and reached for his coat. Giving Holmes a peculiar look, he walked toward the door. Then, turning, he said, 'But how could you know the gentleman's name, Mr Holmes? No report of the incident has appeared in any paper.'

Sherlock Holmes lay back in his chair and pressed his fingertips together. 'Well, now. Shall we say that it is a professional secret, Chief Inspector.'

Lestrade turned once more to leave. A

question now occurred to me.

'Lestrade,' I said, 'how did you know that Mr Holmes had returned to Baker Street?'

A glint appeared in the policeman's eyes. 'Shall we say that is also a professional secret, Doctor Watson. Good day, gentlemen.'

Sherlock Holmes and I lunched at Maison du Bossis, where we consumed a sole each and a bottle of Chablis between us.

'Holmes,' I said tentatively. 'Do you wish to talk about your brother?'

'You would like to hear something about him?'

'Indeed,' I replied. 'He seemed to be a most interesting man.'

Holmes made a wry smile. A far-away look came into his eyes. Clearly the mists of time were parting before his gaze. 'My mother died whilst I was very young,' said he, 'and my father was away from home a good deal. So it was to Mycroft that I looked for guidance. Whilst we were both still young men, my father was killed in an accident. Father's death posed Mycroft a pretty problem. Just a few weeks before the accident he had sat and passed the Civil Service entrance examination and had been offered a post at the department of internal revenue. It was the first rung on what everyone agreed was the ladder to certain success.

'Yet my brother's main concern was for me. I had just turned twelve. His solution was to send me to a boarding school.'

'An experience which is not always a pleasant one,' I said.

'Fortunately, Mycroft made an excellent choice.' Holmes drained his glass, but for a moment he thoughtfully retained it before his face. 'Mycroft, meanwhile, had become every bit as successful as predicted. Although he received few promotions, he made himself indispensable to the Cabinet. Notwithstanding, he constantly helped and watched over me until such time as I was able to stand on my own two feet. It is to my brother, Mycroft, that I owe everything.'

I patted Holmes gently on the arm. 'I completely understand. I am dreadfully sorry, old fellow.'

Holmes pushed back his chair and stood up. 'Well, Doctor, enough of the past. We have to face the future, be it ever so bleak.'

When Sherlock Holmes and I returned to 221B Baker Street, Mrs Blair was waiting for us. 'Oh, Doctor Watson, Mr Holmes,' she said. 'A lady called for you about half an hour ago. As it was such a cold day I asked her to wait upstairs. I hope I done right.'

'Has this lady been here before, Mrs Blair? I asked.

'Oh yes, sir. She was round here twice last week when you was in Sussex.'

'Very good,' I said. 'Perhaps you would be kind enough in a few minutes to send us up some tea.'

Mrs Blair looked expressively at me for a moment and it seemed as if she was about to speak, then she checked herself and in the end, she only muttered, 'Yes, Doctor Watson.'

Our visitor had been sitting by the fire, but she jumped up and ran to us when we entered the room. 'Oh, Doctor Watson, at last!' she cried.

'You are Mrs Andrews?'

'Yes, but...'

'Doctor Jacks has written to me about you. He tells me that you are seeking my advice.'

'Oh yes, yes. I understand that you have often helped others who have come to you asking for assistance.'

I threw my coat and hat onto a chair and led the young woman back to the fire. She was shivering, but whether because of the cold or agitation I could not tell. Holmes, meanwhile, sat by the table with a slightly sardonic smile on his face. 'Please, Mrs

Andrews, sit down... It is true that I played a small part in giving succour to those who sought it. Although I have to tell you mine was not the mind that parted the mists of confusion and saw into the heart of the matter.'

Sherlock Holmes laughed out loud. 'Well said, Watson,' he cried.

Mrs Andrews looked at Holmes. 'Please, sir. I do not know your name, but do not ridicule someone who speaks so nobly.'

Holmes bowed low. 'Madam,' he said soberly. 'You will forgive me. It was the doctor's description of myself which I found so amusing.'

Again, Mrs Andrews jumped to her feet. 'Then you are Mr Sherlock Holmes?' she exclaimed.

'Your humble servant.'

Mrs Andrews turned once more to face me. 'Forgive me, Doctor Watson, but if your friend truly is Sherlock Holmes, then my position is not a hopeless one.'

'Truly this is he,' I said. 'But you must know that Mr Holmes has retired.'

Our visitor reached for her bag, opened it and took out a small roll of five-pound notes. 'If it is a matter of money, I have here, one hundred and fifty pounds which will

34

pay for your services.'

Mrs Andrews gazed expectantly at Holmes who gave a gentle sigh of resignation. 'Very well, Mrs Andrews, I will do what I can.'

'You will help me, thank heaven.'

Once again, as in years gone past, Sherlock Holmes sat in the old armchair with the horsehair stuffing falling out, his eyes closed and his fingertips drawn together. 'Now, Mrs Andrews, if you will relay the events exactly as they occurred then, perhaps, I may be able to glean something which the police have missed.'

'Perhaps, Mr Holmes, if I may enquire exactly the extent of your knowledge about my situation?'

'Very well,' said Holmes. 'Your general accent betrays you as being a Lancastrian. Indeed, certain peculiarities in your speech lead me to the conclusion that you are native to an area not more than twenty miles from the town of Rochdale.

'You have moved up in the world, no doubt through your marriage, but you have not compromised your independent nature.

'You do not desire to appear in the company of the middle-class matrons in whose midst you live, and your husband has been kidnapped. Apart from these obvious facts, I can tell you very little. Oh, you have very recently suffered a small accident in which you dropped your handbag.'

'Well, Mr Holmes,' said our visitor. 'Your reputation is well deserved. There is one thing, however. Although I can understand your reasoning when you describe me so fully, I do not see how you could know that when walking down Baker Street an hour ago an incident occurred which caused me to drop my handbag.'

Sherlock Holmes sat forward in his chair and picked up the handbag. 'If I may explain,' he said, handing the lady her bag. 'Please open it, Mrs Andrews.'

Mrs Andrews did as she was bid.

'Well, Watson. Do you detect anything?'

'Do you mean apart from the strong smell of Eau de Cologne?' I asked.

'It is the very smell of Cologne to which I allude.' Holmes again looked at our visitor. 'You say that an incident caused you to drop your bag, Mrs Andrews?'

'Yes, a man came running down Baker Street and crashed into me. My bag was knocked to the ground and some of the contents were spilled into the gutter. He was most apologetic. He turned his back on me and retrieved my bag. For a moment I was

36

concerned that he would make off with it.'

'Indeed,' I replied. 'With one hundred and fifty pounds contained within.'

'But the money remained untouched. It seems that the only casualty was my Cologne bottle.'

'Which Holmes identified when you opened your bag,' I said.

'You are certain that nothing was taken?' said Holmes.

Mrs Andrews briefly inspected the contents of her bag; suddenly she gave a cry of anguish. 'My keys! They are gone.'

Sherlock Holmes jumped to his feet and snatched his hat and coat from the peg. 'Mrs Andrews,' he cried. 'Your keys were the object of this accident. What is your address?'

Our visitor looked slightly bewildered by this sudden change of events, but she answered promptly. 'I live at 81 St John's Wood High Street.'

'Very good. Come, Watson, we must hurry. The miscreant has a head start on us, but perhaps he is still in residence. Mrs Andrews, you will wait here until we return.'

The lady was not inclined to obey, however, for she stood up with a determined look in her brown eyes. 'It is my house this scoundrel has violated. I refuse to sit by calmly and do nothing.'

'Very well,' said Holmes. 'Come if you must, Mrs Andrews, but I warn you, there may be violence.'

Holmes ran down the stairs and into the street below, whilst I put on my hat and coat, slipped my service revolver into my pocket then escorted the lady downstairs.

The carriage rattled through the busy streets of the Metropolis. Along Grove Road we flew, past St John's Wood Church and into the High Street.

Sherlock Holmes was out of the cab and running down the pavement. Mrs Andrews and I followed as quickly as we were able. Moments later he reached the steps of number 81. It was a large three-storey building which had been converted into offices below and living accommodation above. Holmes pulled at the latch. The door remained firmly closed.

'Have you a spare door key?' he said hoarsely, his breathing harsh.

'My next door neighbour keeps a key,' the lady replied, 'I will get it from her.'

'Then hurry, Mrs Andrews. Hurry.'

A few moments later Mrs Andrews returned with the spare key. Holmes turned to me. 'Now, Doctor. You will enter the house with Mrs Andrews, whilst I shall operate from the rear of the property. If the fellow is still in residence perhaps you will frighten him into my waiting arms.'

Holmes opened the side gate and a moment later he had vanished. I took Mrs Andrews by the arm and led her up the steps to the front door.

'Please keep behind me at all times,' I said. 'If there is danger it is better that I should face it.'

Quickly I turned the key and threw open the door. There was a terrific bang as the door hit the wall. But from elsewhere in the house not a sound could be heard.

The stairs were before us. Three doors were around us. Mrs Andrews whispered into my ear. 'The door on the left is Hunter's private office, the door on the right is the planning office, and the door at the foot of the stairs leads to the old kitchens and the rear entrance. Only the kitchen door should be unlocked.'

I tried the handle to Mr Andrews's office. It was unlocked. I pulled from my pocket my service revolver, a companion of so many excursions into tight corners. The door I threw open. The room was empty and there were few signs of damage; only a glass cabinet had been forced and the desk drawers had been broken into.

The planning office had fared less well. There was little sign of damage, but plans had been scattered to the four corners of the room. Then, from behind, there came the creak of a floorboard. I spun around ready to ward off an attacker.

'My dear fellow,' said Sherlock Holmes calmly, 'please do not shoot.'

'You have discovered something?' I asked.

'Indeed, there are several signs of a hasty exit. It is probable that the fellow bolted when he heard our arrival.'

Holmes also held up something that clinked and tinkled.

'My keys,' cried Mrs Andrews, 'where did you find them, Mr Holmes?'

'Close by the back steps. The fellow dropped them in his haste.'

After a few minutes, Mrs Andrews was able to report that nothing upstairs had been touched.

'This is a decidedly odd affair, Holmes,' I said, 'we appear to be in pursuit of a felon who ignores a great deal of money when stealing some keys, who then spends some considerable time rummaging through offices when upstairs a veritable *Aladdin's Cave* may be awaiting him. It make no sense.'

Sherlock Holmes curled his bottom lip and chewed reflectively at it for a moment. Then without a word he began a minute examination of the ground floor. For fully fifteen minutes Mrs Andrews and I watched him closely inspecting the front door, crawling around the hall floor and striding in and out of the offices.

'Our man clearly entered by the front door,' he said at last, 'see here, Watson. There are some fresh scratches on the lock. He had no indication as to which key fitted which lock and tried each one until the correct key opened the door. In his haste he caused the damage; unlike Mrs Andrews and yourself, Doctor, the miscreant did not stop to wipe his feet. Observe, his first step was in the direction of Mr Andrews's office, his second step was towards the main office. At this stage he was undecided in his next move. There is a third footprint, however, which clearly indicated his decision to begin with Mr Andrews's office. There, Watson. It is faint, but it is just visible on the threshold.'

'Can you ascertain how he searched the office?' I said as we followed Holmes into the room.

Holmes smiled. 'My dear fellow. Neither this office nor the main one was searched. The fellow knew exactly the item or items he wished to steal and he also knew exactly where to find his prize.'

'But what of the mess?' cried Mrs Andrews.

'It was made to conceal the fact that something particular and significant has been taken.'

'But you cannot be certain, surely, Holmes?'

'Look around you, Watson. What do you see?'

'Drawers broken open, a cabinet in disarray and some papers on the floor. All the signs of a burglary.'

'As I have oft remarked, Doctor, you look but you do not see. Look again. The drawers have indeed been broken open, but the contents lie untouched. The cabinet is also vandalized, but the books are sitting tidily on their shelves. The papers have been dropped almost in a pile.'

'What of the mess in the main office?'

'If you will observe,' said Holmes, striding across the hall, 'there is no physical damage to any of the desks or cupboards. The papers have been randomly scattered to simulate a hasty search. No, Watson, this is no ordinary burglary, something special has been removed.'

Before I could comment on his remarkable piece of detection, Holmes was marching back into the hall. He called out to Mrs Andrews to look and see if any particular thing was missing.

'Come along, Watson. There is something further I wish to show you,' he cried as he departed for the kitchen. 'Look at the back door. What do you see?'

'The lock has been broken.'

'But by what sort of tool has it been broken?'

I closely inspected the lock. Many times had I seen a broken lock, but there was something strange here. 'This is most odd, Holmes. The damage is slight but the lock has been ripped off as effectively as if a jemmy had been used on it. I do not know of any tool which would do such an efficient job, yet cause so little peripheral damage. Can you throw any light on the matter?'

'I believe so. Only once before have I come across such a tool. It is a specialist tool called a Barrington pin-hammer. It resembles a claw hammer but the claw is slim and fine, rather resembling an ice-pick.'

'This pin-hammer. What is its role?'

'It is used in the making and unmaking of large safes and some strong rooms,' said Holmes. 'It is a specialist tool for driving home or removing the pins which anchor safe doors to their hinges. It weighs about two pounds and is usually made of the finest steel for strength and durability.'

From within the house came a woman's cry. 'Mrs Andrews,' I said, 'I had quite forgotten her.'

'Hurry, Watson,' cried Holmes, 'the lady is obviously alarmed.'

Sherlock Holmes and I quickly returned to the hall where we discovered Mrs Andrews alone but somewhat upset. She was wringing her hands in agitation.

'My dear lady,' said Holmes, 'what ails you?'

'Oh, Mr Holmes. It is my husband's tool set. It has been taken.'

I was somewhat bemused by this sudden outburst because I had previously regarded Mrs Andrews as a particularly self-possessed young woman. But to witness her distress over a set of tools struck me as strange, even bizarre. 'My dear Mrs Andrews,' I said. 'Please calm yourself. Surely, the loss of a tool set does not warrant such an outburst?'

Holmes took the young woman by one

44

elbow and gently propelled her back into her husband's office. His voice was soothing, yet somehow insistent. 'Am I right in supposing that your husband's tool set was far from the ordinary kind, Mrs Andrews?'

Mrs Andrews sat on an adjacent office chair. 'That is so, Mr Holmes. My husband was in possession of a specialist set of Barrington tools. Only he and I know the whereabouts of their hiding place and yet they have been stolen.'

The eyes of Sherlock Holmes took on an almost incandescent glow in the afternoon light. 'Capital, capital!' he exclaimed. 'The whole picture emerges; Mrs Andrews, could Doctor Watson and myself impose upon you for a little afternoon tea?'

The lady, although much confused at the gayness of his tone, readily consented to the request of Sherlock Holmes.

'You have solved the case, Holmes?' I ventured.

'Not solved, Doctor. But I believe, however, that much of the mist which has shrouded this matter has now lifted.'

Tea was taken in the lady's neat and tastefully furnished sitting room. Holmes sipped his tea and nodded appreciatively.

'Excellent.'

'Thank you, Mr Holmes.'

'Now, Holmes, perhaps you can help Mrs Andrews and myself in understanding this matter,' I said.

'Indeed,' said Holmes. 'It was you, yourself, who pointed out the strangeness of the fact that keys were taken and money was left untouched.'

'A common thief would never be so choosy,' I said.

'Quite so, Watson, but, Mrs Andrews, before I elucidate further perhaps you would be kind enough to tell me something about your husband and the events that surrounded his kidnapping.'

'You believe that these two events are somehow connected, Mr Holmes?'

'I do,' said Holmes, firmly.

Mrs Andrews stood up and walked across the room. She opened a drawer in the large mahogany sideboard and took out a silver locket. 'Here, Mr Holmes. This locket contains the only photograph I have of my husband.'

Holmes took the locket, briefly glanced at the contents, then handed it to me. The photograph was of a young man in his thirties. He was clean-shaven and had a veritable mop of black curly hair. It was, however his eyes which caught my attention. They were black and piercing.

'I call them gypsy eyes, Doctor Watson,' said Mrs Andrews, apparently reading my mind. 'Sometimes I think he is more Heathcliff than Hunter.'

Holmes said, 'Mrs Andrews, if you would be so kind...'

'Yes, of course. My husband was born in Henley-on-Thames, the youngest son of Sir Walter Andrews, the industrialist. Hunter inherited two thousand pounds from his father's estate some ten years ago. He was also fortunate enough to inherit his father's business acumen. He is now the owner of two foundries, one in Croydon, which makes bells and the other is in Pimlico, which makes the specialist tools which he uses in the other part of his business, the one that manufactures safes and strong-rooms.'

Sherlock Holmes jumped from his chair and rubbed his hands together excitedly. 'Now, Mrs Andrews, perhaps you would care to exactly describe your husband's kidnapping.'

Mrs Andrews sat with the silver locket in her hands. 'It was on March the first, at about ten o'clock in the morning, when Hunter called up the stairs to me asking if I would care for a trip into the country the next day. He had just received a communication from a client in Tring who wished to discuss the possibility of a new safe in his office.'

'Did Mr Andrews divulge the name of this client?' said Holmes.

'A Mr Porter, a gentleman whom I have met on several previous occasions. It was as I came to the head of the stairs to reply to his question, that two men came crashing through the front door, roughly attacked Hunter and dragged him away.'

'I ran down the stairs to see what had become of my husband. All I could see was the two men pushing him into a motor car, which roared into life and sped off down the High Street in the direction of Regent's Park.'

'And you have had no contact with your husband or his kidnappers?' I said.

'No, Doctor Watson,' said our hostess, 'nothing at all.'

Sherlock Holmes gave a little laugh. 'Does it not seem strange, Watson, that the kidnappers have yet to communicate their demands? Mr Andrews has been in their hands for over a week, yet there has been no message.'

'Indeed, but for the life of me I can see no reason why.'

'Ah, Watson. There is an excellent reason: Mr Andrews was kidnapped not for a ransom, he was abducted for his specialist knowledge.'

'Of course. It also explains why today's events have appeared to be so bizarre.'

'Exactly. Last week they took the man, this week they have returned for his tools.'

Mrs Andrews clutched the sleeve of Sherlock Holmes and looked earnestly at him. 'Does this mean that my husband may be soon returned to me?'

'I believe that when his task is completed he will be released.'

'Oh, Mr Holmes, you bring me hope. For the first time in a week of constant worry I can be optimistic about my husband's safe return.'

Sherlock Holmes stood up and retrieved his hat from the dresser. 'For the present there is little more I can do here,' he said. 'Goodbye, Mrs Andrews. I will be in touch.'

As we descended the three steps into St John's Wood High Street, Holmes reached into an inside pocket and retrieved a small bronze coin, which he handed to me. 'Here, Doctor. What do you make of this?'

'A foreign coin, Holmes,' I said, examining it closely. 'But it is inscribed in an alphabet which I do not recall ever learning. It resembles Greek.'

'Excellent, Watson. What else do you deduce?'

'Well,' I said, 'the head upon the coin resembles strongly that of His Majesty the King, but I do not know of any country in the Empire that would be allowed to have anything but English upon its coinage.'

Holmes smiled benignly, 'My dear fellow. As usual you have misled yourself. This coin is not Greek and the head is not His Majesty's.'

Holmes smiled. 'The alphabet is Cyrillic and the head on the coin is that of the Tsar of Russia. It is a fifty-kopeck piece. It was lying on the back steps of the house we have just left.'

'But what would a Russian want with Mr Hunter Andrews?'

'That, my dear Watson, is something we shall have to investigate,' said Holmes, returning the coin to his inside pocket. 'There is, however, little more to be done today. I therefore suggest that we adjourn to the Royal Albert Hall, where Lizio is conducting Bruckner's ninth. A morose symphony, but one suitable for my present mood,' he smiled sadly. 'If you would care to accompany me, Watson, we could then retire to Maison du Bossis for supper.'

THREE

It was a little after eleven a.m.; the morning papers, having failed to excite the interest of Sherlock Holmes, lay strewn across our sitting room floor. As for the man himself he sat perched on the sill of the window overlooking Baker Street.

'Holmes?'

'Yes, my dear fellow?'

'You believe, that Mr Hunter Andrews will be safely released?'

'Providing that the kidnappers took care not to let him discover their identities, I believe so; logic would dictate it to be so. No matter when the constabulary discovers the crime, what can he tell them? That he was abducted by two unknown men who never revealed their identities, who took him to an unknown destination, who forced him to participate in a criminal activity and then returned him to his home? They would have little to fear from Mr Andrews.'

'But you cannot be certain?'

'There is very little in life that is certain, Watson. However, answer me this. Would you have told the lady that criminals often kill mindlessly and callously, that her husband's life may hang upon the thread of some villain's caprice?'

'No, indeed!' I said warmly. 'Although she is in every way a splendid young woman, Mrs Andrews can only be expected to endure so much. She must be allowed to retain her belief in the safe return of her husband.'

'Exactly,' said Holmes.

Our conversation was at this moment rudely interrupted by the sudden arrival of General James Wilton. He was flushed with excitement. 'Mr Holmes, John', he cried. 'I am sorry to break in upon you like this, but the Cabinet Office has recently received a diplomatic pouch from Italy which contained a letter from Mr Mycroft Holmes, along with medical evidence of his death.'

Holmes stood bolt upright by the fire. It was with the greatest of effort that he composed himself sufficiently to speak. His voice was harsh and rasping. 'You have the letter with you, General?'

'I have, sir.' The old soldier opened the black briefcase he was carrying and took out some papers. 'Here.'

Holmes took them with trembling fingers. The letter he took out of the envelope. The medical report he handed to me. The letter reads:

My dear Lord Falmouth,

Please forgive the precipitous manner in the way in which I made my exit from the conference. It was the result of a particularly unhappy meeting with an Italian carriage.

The doctor at the clinic assures me that I have nothing more than a little internal bruising and that in a few days I will be back on my feet again.

Mycroft
Bixio Clinic, Rome.

'It is dated the third day of March 1912. The day he died', said Holmes, his voice dropping almost to a whisper.

I could do no more than watch helplessly as Holmes almost cradled the letter in his hands. His long tapering fingers caressed the words, so carelessly written by his dead brother. For a moment, I imagined that there was a moistening of his eyes as once again he read the note. Then the moment passed. Sherlock Holmes laid down the letter and gazed steadily at me. 'Cast a cold eye on death, Watson.'

'Indeed.'

'Now then, old fellow, what does the doctor's report say?'

'Well,' said I, glancing over the document, 'Although it is written in Italian, there is sufficient in the language, which has Latin roots, for me to discern that the cause of death of Mr Holmes was peritonitis after appendicitis, which occurred because of a heavy blow to the abdomen.'

'That would be so,' interrupted the general. 'You will recall, Mr Holmes, that your brother's note spoke of an accident with a carriage.'

I folded up the report and handed it back to Sherlock Holmes. 'In a nutshell, Holmes, your brother died from a ruptured appendix.'

It was at this juncture that a sudden and incredible change came over Sherlock Holmes. 'Ha, ha!' he cried. 'A burst appendix, eh? My dear fellow,' and Holmes continued to laugh in the most hilarious, almost hysterical, manner.

General Wilton took me by the arm. 'What

is it, John? Has Mr Holmes taken leave of his senses?'

Holmes, by now, was laughing almost fit to burst. He also began to clap his hands and dance to some inaudible tune played by some invisible band.

'It is the shock, James. Mr Holmes is temporarily suffering from hysteria. Perhaps you had better leave whilst I attempt to calm him.'

The general took up his case and hat and swiftly made for the door. 'Goodbye, John. Perhaps I shall see you tomorrow.' As the door closed behind our visitor, I turned once again to face my friend. At once he was his old self again. The wild look had vanished and in its place was an expression I know only too well, a look of uncompromising determination.

'General Wilton has gone?'

'Yes. I heard him departing just as quickly as his legs would carry him.'

'Excellent! Now we have little time to lose.'

'Holmes!' I cried in exasperation. 'Would you mind telling me what exactly is going on?'

'There is some devilry afoot here, Watson. Something dark and sinister is occurring and I mean to discover the source and root it out.'

'But Holmes...'

'My dear fellow, I am so sorry. My recent actions must have both baffled and unnerved you. You have my deepest regrets.'

'You have certainly unnerved General Wilton,' I said. 'For myself, I perceive that it was all an act, but for the life of me, I cannot understand your motive.'

Sherlock Holmes moved over to the sideboard and quickly produced a brandy and soda, which, in spite of the early hour, I gratefully accepted.

'Perhaps, Doctor, you will understand, when I tell you I believe that my brother is not dead.'

'Mycroft alive? But how?'

'You will recall that in 1902, just before the coronation, His Majesty King Edward fell prey to appendicitis?'

'Yes, of course. The celebrations had to be postponed until he was fully recovered.'

'It was a mere two weeks before his Majesty's illness that my brother suffered from the same ailment. As a medical man, Watson, you must know that the appendix does not grow back again.'

'And your brother, therefore, cannot twice

suffer from appendicitis.'

'Exactly. Mycroft is alive.'

The certainty in his voice began to sway me. Sherlock Holmes never stated something to be factual, unless there was comprehensive and overwhelming evidence to hand.

'But how can you be certain, Holmes?'

Holmes raised his left hand and began ticking off the points he made with his right index finger. 'One, Mycroft reported the accident to be of a minor nature. If the accident had indeed been more severe he could not have written the note. Two, the accident as we know did not result in appendicitis, which obviously could not arise. The clinic is clearly lying.'

'Mycroft may have died from other causes?'

'I return to the accident, Watson. Why did the clinic simply not state that he had died as a result of the accident? Why embellish a simple fact? It was an excellent opportunity to report a simple straightforward death, which would not raise any questions. It was, however, fortunate that the clinic reported the cause of my brother's death to be the only illness from which I knew he could not suffer.'

I smiled. 'Well, perhaps you are right. But

what if Mycroft has simply been quietly done away with?'

Holmes laughed. 'Murdered? We are dealing with politicians and government officials. They are not villains and cut-throats.'

'What of the Cosa Nostra?' I ventured.

'The Cosa Nostra are a society who involve themselves in extortion and they do not operate beyond the confines of Sicily and southern Italy.'

'Then we must assume that Mycroft is alive and being held prisoner.'

'Indeed.'

'But where is he hidden?'

'I have no doubt that he is incarcerated at the clinic.'

'But for how long?'

'Ah, well. That is a question I cannot so easily answer,' said Holmes as he sank wearily into his chair.

'Perhaps you will be asked to replace your brother at the conference. Sir Arthur Richardson hinted as much when he visited you the other day. That is always assuming he does not by now think you completely mad.'

Sherlock Holmes thoughtfully rubbed his chin. His long narrow face bore an expression of deep concentration. He snapped his fingers; clearly an idea had occurred to him.

A smile came creeping over his face. 'Ah, Watson. I sincerely trust that he will.'

'Holmes, what do you mean?'

Sherlock Holmes sat forward in his chair. His knees almost touching mine, he spread his hands out before him. 'If Sir Arthur cannot rely on the services of the other Holmes, he may ask for a postponement of the conference until I am sufficiently recovered or until he can find another who can be relied upon to successfully represent His Majesty's government. Either way there will inevitably be a delay.'

'You mean to lead Sir Arthur into the belief that you have become unstable?'

'Unhinged, by the terrible news of my brother's death.'

I sat back into my chair and took in a deep breath. 'But, to what end, Holmes?'

'Whilst Sir Arthur and His Majesty's government believe me to be unwell, I may be able to get to the bottom of this tangled web of intrigue.'

'What is your plan?' I enquired.

'In two days you will announce that because of my present incapacity, I will be taken to my villa in Sussex. After a further day's delay, you will issue a note, which will say that, as my condition has not improved, you are moving me to a nearby nursing home, where the conditions are more conducive to my recovery.'

'But how will your supposed mental instability assist your brother?'

Holmes smiled thinly. 'It will surely convince his captors that immediate discovery is unlikely. Supposing that they have nothing to fear from the investigative machinations of Sherlock Holmes, or indeed anyone else, they will delay accordingly the decision, what must be done about Mycroft.'

'What if they decide to move Mycroft to a more secure place? Somewhere they can quietly dispose of him, at their leisure?'

'That is why we must act swiftly. News of my incapacity will reach them within twenty-four hours. By then, we must be well on our way to Rome.'

'Rome?' I said with some surprise.

'Indeed, to the Bixio Clinic to be precise, Doctor.'

'Very well, Holmes,' I said. 'In that case I had better make the arrangements to have you committed.'

It was later that afternoon. I was walking along Baker Street in the direction of 221B, having just returned from making the necessary arrangements for the nursing home with my colleague Jacks. I had sworn Jacks to secrecy. The plan so carefully arranged by Sherlock Holmes could brook no interference; fortunately, a confidence communicated to a doctor is as sacrosanct as one entrusted to a priest in the confessional.

A man detached himself from a shop front and spoke to me. 'Doctor Watson. Is it true?'

'Why, Lestrade. Good afternoon. Is what true?'

The detective cleared his throat and shuffled his feet. 'Is it true about Mr Holmes?' he said.

'Mr Holmes?' I replied.

Lestrade drew closer and spoke almost in a whisper. 'I am referring to the rumour that Mr Holmes has gone off his head, sir.'

I was frankly astounded that news of the supposed illness of Sherlock Holmes had been broadcast quite so quickly. I drew the detective aside. 'Is this news common currency, Lestrade?' I asked. 'How did you come by the information?'

Lestrade gave a chuckle. 'Hardly, sir,' he tapped his long nose with his left forefinger. 'And as I told you yesterday, I too have my professional secrets.'

'The street is not the place for loose talk,

Lestrade. Perhaps we should continue this conversation upstairs in my rooms where any discourse on the sanity or otherwise of Mr Holmes cannot be overheard by the casual loafer.'

The detective's thin weaselly face showed surprise at the warmth of my tone. 'H'm. Beg your pardon, Doctor Watson. Perhaps I talked out of turn. You are quite right. Matters so serious should not be openly discussed.'

A few moments later Lestrade and I were at the door of 221B Baker Street. I took him by the arm and issued a warning. 'Mr Holmes may not be pleased to see you, Chief Inspector. If you would be kind enough to wait in the hall, I shall go upstairs and ascertain his mood.'

Lestrade gave a start and answered me in a most agitated voice. 'He is not likely to be violent, Doctor?'

I could hardly suppress my desire to laugh, but I replied in the most sober manner. 'My dear Lestrade. Surely a man such as yourself, who has faced untold numbers of vicious criminals and has oft laughed in the face of danger, will not baulk at the prospect of meeting a sick man?'

'No, sir. I suppose not,' he said faintly.

'Capital. Now please wait here and I shall return shortly.'

I found Sherlock Holmes sitting quietly by the fire. In his hand was Mycroft's letter to Lord Falmouth. The letter was swiftly transferred to the pocket of his dressing gown, however.

'Ah, Watson. You have returned. Have the necessary arrangements been made?'

'They have.'

'Excellent.'

'There is a visitor for you, Holmes. It is Lestrade. He has somehow or other become acquainted with rumours of your condition.'

Sherlock Holmes looked sharply at me. 'How the deuce did he get a hold of the news?'

'He is downstairs. Perhaps you would like to quiz him on the matter?'

'Indeed. Ask him up, Watson.'

I turned and opened the door. Stepping out onto the landing, I hailed the detective waiting below. 'Chief Inspector, you may come up.'

When I once again turned my gaze on the person of Sherlock Holmes, I observed that a remarkable change had come over him. He now appeared to be shrunken and subdued under the burden of a depressive illness.

Indeed, he was hardly recognizable as the man with whom I had so very recently been conversing.

Lestrade entered, hat in hand. His face bore a mixture of suppressed terror and extreme consternation at the apparent condition of his host. 'Mr Holmes. I have come to see if there is anything I can do for you,' he said untruthfully.

'My dear Lestrade,' said Holmes wearily, his voice barely rising above a whisper. 'You are most kind. No, there is nothing you can do for me. I am too far-gone for the assistance of my friends, no matter how kind and solicitous. It is my mind you see. Dear Watson here tells me that I am ... what was it, old fellow... Ah yes. I am unsound in mind.'

Lestrade took a step back and glanced nervously in my direction.

'Please do not distress yourself, Chief Inspector,' I said. 'It is a condition which will soon pass.'

Holmes made a feeble attempt to rise from his chair, but collapsed in a tangled heap on the floor before the fire. I ran forward to assist him.

'Quickly, Lestrade,' I cried, 'give me a hand here.'

Reluctantly, the detective moved across the

room and assisted me in helping Holmes back into his chair. Holmes, his eyes hot with a feverish glow, grabbed Lestrade by the sleeve. 'My condition is not generally known, is it, Lestrade?' he demanded.

The policeman, whose whole demeanour presently resembled that of a startled rabbit trapped in the gaze of a hungry weasel, was barely able to reply. 'Oh no, sir,' he croaked. 'I believe that it is only the Cabinet Office and myself who know.'

'What's that,' I cried. 'What has the Cabinet Office to do with all this?'

The grip on Lestrade's arm tightened. Holmes affixed him with a glare which would have unnerved the bravest of men. Lestrade, however, did not fall into the category.

'Please, Doctor Watson. Ask him to leave go,' he exclaimed.

'Mr Holmes will let you go if you answer me truthfully. Why did the Cabinet Office contact you? Mr Holmes will be happier in his mind if he knows that his illness is not common gossip throughout the Metropolitan Police Force.'

'I can assure you, sir, it is not so. The only reason for my knowledge of Mr Holmes's illness came because of a telephone call received from General Wilton who confided in me his concerns. He had recently witnessed Mr Holmes acting in a most eccentric manner, and requested that I undertake an investigation on his behalf.'

Holmes smiled wolfishly at the frightened policeman. 'And only General Wilton and yourself are privy to this matter, Lestrade?' he said.

'Oh yes, sir. Only myself and the general.'

Sherlock Holmes released his vice-like grip and Lestrade jumped away as if he had been the recipient of an electric shock.

'Thank you, Chief Inspector,' Holmes said calmly. 'That means a great deal to me.'

Lestrade took me by the arm and almost dragged me to the door. When we were safely returned to the landing he cried out in a shaky falsetto voice: 'He's quite mad, Doctor Watson. It's my opinion that Mr Holmes is a danger to all those who come near him. I would send him away somewhere as quick as maybe, if I were you.'

I patted Lestrade on the shoulder and smiled. 'Do not concern yourself, old fellow. Mr Holmes will not harm me. I am the only person in whom he will put his trust. Believe me, Lestrade, all will be well.'

The detective made his way back down the stairs. As he reached the front door he

66

shouted a parting retort. 'Good luck, Doctor. Sooner you than me. He is clearly quite mad and I shall be telling the general just that.'

'Goodbye, Lestrade,' I cried. 'Thank you.'

Sherlock Holmes appeared in the doorway as the street door banged behind the departing detective. 'Excellent!' he cried. 'Lestrade will certainly broadcast my sad decline into madness. We can be assured of the news spreading across London like an epidemic of influenza and by this time tomorrow the newspapers will be on our doorstep seeking information.'

'Indeed,' I said. 'If that is the case, then perhaps I had better prepare a statement for them.'

Holmes laughed. 'Good old Lestrade.'

I took Holmes by the arm and propelled him back into his seat. 'Now, sir, as your physician, I prescribe a glass of something warming and intoxicating. It is for medicinal purposes only, you understand.'

Holmes smiled. 'Indeed, Doctor. That is an excellent prescription to which I will cheerfully adhere.'

After supper Sherlock Holmes and I sat quietly reading. Holmes, a self-confessed literary philistine, was deep in a lurid re-creation of the infamous Whitechapel murders of the 1880s, whilst I was engaged in Professor Whitehead's study of the plays of William Shakespeare.

I had just finished reading the professor's scholarly remarks on the androgyny of characters in *Twelfth Night*, when there was a loud ringing of the front bell.

'Ah, a visitor,' said Holmes snapping shut his book. 'It is evidently someone who is rather agitated,' he remarked as the bell was sounded for a second time.

Then there came a piercing scream from the downstairs hallway. Holmes and I sprang to our feet.

'Was that not Mrs Blair?' I exclaimed.

'Undoubtedly.'

Holmes threw open our sitting room door and pitched himself down the stairs. Deciding that owing to my arthritic condition, I would follow more sedately. I arrived in the hallway just in time to witness Sherlock Holmes on his knees cradling the head of a fallen man. 'Quickly, Watson,' he cried. 'This man needs your assistance.'

Brushing past the quivering form of Mrs Blair I swiftly examined the man. I judged him to be somewhere between fifty and sixty years of age. He wore the unmistakable garb of a seaman. He was in a semi-conscious state and at first I thought him to be drunk, then a discovery of a more serious and sinister nature caused me to cry out.

'Great Scott, Holmes. This man has been stabbed!'

Again Mrs Blair began to cry. Sherlock Holmes stood up and took her by the shoulders. 'Madam, if you would be so kind as to clear everything away from your kitchen table, Doctor Watson will treat this gentleman there.'

Mrs Blair made a tearful exit, calling out for her son George to lend a hand.

The man was beginning to perspire heavily. He muttered some incoherent sounds.

'Do not tax yourself, sir,' I said gently. 'My friend and I will soon make you more comfortable.'

A few moments later we laid our strange visitor on Mrs Blair's kitchen table.

I turned to young George and ordered him to run upstairs and retrieve my doctor's bag. Mrs Blair I asked to boil the water and prepare some strips of clean cloth.

'Now, Holmes,' I said, 'let us get the man's coat off. Then his jumper and shirt.'

With the removal of the man's shirt, I was

able to observe the extent of his wounds. There were three superficial stab wounds to his abdomen, but as far as I could tell there was no damage to any vital organ. Clearly he had lost quite a lot of blood. George returned with my bag and I was soon able to clean and dress the wounds.

Then quite suddenly the man opened his eyes and spoke directly to me. 'Mr Holmes. I must speak to Mr Sherlock Holmes.'

Holmes stepped forward. 'I am Holmes,' he said quietly.

'Oh, Mr Holmes. Thank goodness I have found you,' he said, the words coming in short staccato bursts.

Holmes took the seaman's hand and pressed it gently. 'How may I help you, sir?'

'I have some information for you,' he whispered. 'There was something I witnessed the other day that I have to tell you about.'

I said, 'Holmes, this man is scarcely well enough to talk. This should wait until he is a little better.'

'No, Doctor Watson,' cried the man. 'There is something I have to get off my chest.'

I sighed and waved my hands in a gesture of futility. Holmes gently squeezed the man's hand. 'Please continue, Mr...?'

'Hockney, Tom Hockney.'

'Please continue, Mr Hockney.'

'I expect that you've guessed I am a seaman. I am just back from a trip to the Mediterranean. I crew with Captain Jefferson on his old coaster, the *Pride of Thanet*.'

'Two days ago we docked at Ramsgate and the captain paid us all off with instructions to be back on board the next night for a midnight sailing to Naples. After I got my pay I went ashore with the rest. It was when I was climbing up the plains of Waterloo that I remembered my watch, I had dropped it during the voyage and had broken it.

'Cursing my own stupidity I retraced my steps and reboarded the ship. Well, I went below deck collecting my watch and had just come up on deck when I saw a large motor car come alongside. There were three men in the vehicle: one seemed to be ill, for the other two literally dragged him on board.

'The captain appeared. He seemed quite upset and complained that if they were bringing onboard a passenger they should do it at night when no one could spot them. The two men said nothing. They just bundled their companion below deck.'

Sherlock Holmes took a cold compress and gently pressed it to Mr Hockney's forehead. 'Was the captain a regular transporter of passengers?'

'Oh, yes. He would often move people in and out of the country.'

'Mm. Excellent; pray continue.'

'The man seemed not to want to be a passenger, because there was much shouting from below and he appeared once more on deck. He was shouting for help, but the two men grabbed him and took him back below.

'This unnerved me a bit. It seemed to me to be as blatant a piece of kidnapping as could be. Perhaps, I thought, it would be as well if I summoned the police.

'But, my feet betrayed me. I tripped as I passed the wheelhouse and the captain heard me. At once he realized that I had heard and seen all. He shouted to the two men that there was a spy on board.

'I picked myself up and ran down the gangway, I could hear the footsteps of the two men running behind me. Fortunately, I was able to jump onto a passing omnibus and escape them. But it was clear that the captain had recognized me and the men would be sent after me.

'I realized that the only sensible course for me was to come to London and seek you out, for the local police station was sure to be watched.

'I took the train from Dumpton Park to Victoria Station. All the way I was in a state of nerves. I was terrified that the men would be on the train as well, but when I got to Victoria there was no one in sight. I relaxed a bit then.

'From Victoria, I came straight round to Baker Street. But the house was empty and not a light was shown.'

'At about what o'clock did you arrive, Mr Hockney?' said Holmes.

'It was just after ten p.m.'

Holmes looked across the table at me. 'We were at supper. That was rather unfortunate.'

Hockney went on. 'I turned away, disappointed that there was nobody home. I didn't quite know what to do next. I resolved to wait until next morning and come back again.'

'But where were you intending to pass the night?'

'I meant to skipper in the park. It was only the one night. I thought it to be the safest place.

'I turned to walk away when I was stopped by a huge man with a black beard. He said, "You are Hockney." Before I could move one way or the other he grabbed me and plunged a knife into my guts. I staggered and he caught me. Then he dragged me along Baker Street. As luck would have it, the street was deserted. I tried to call out, but I began to feel weak. Then I passed out.

'When I came back to myself, I was lying on some sacking close to the edge of a large sewer outlet into the Thames. The man was standing over me. He was holding what seemed to be pieces of wood which he began to shove into my pockets; I realised by the weight of these objects that they were made of lead.

'Then the man turned away and began uncoiling some rope. It was plain enough that he was planning a watery grave for me.

'My shirt and jumper were soaked in blood and I felt lightheaded, but I knew that it was now or never if I was to save my life. I reached into my right-hand jacket pocket and pulled out the lead weight. As he turned around and bent over me in order to tie me up, I lashed out with all my strength.

'I caught him a smashing blow in the face. As he stumbled and fell, I rose to my feet and ran from there as fast as I could go.

'I don't know how far I staggered or to which hole I bolted. I ran down some alley and fell into a woodshed. I passed out again and only came to myself an hour ago. This time I managed to get to Baker Street unmolested. Maybe I killed the man. But I did it, Mr Holmes, I did it.'

'So you did, Mr Hockney, so you did.'

'Now, Holmes,' I said. 'He must rest. These wounds may be serious enough to need hospital treatment, only I believe it to be unwise to move him just yet. I will give Mr Hockney a little morphine to help him rest and perhaps young George will be kind enough to help us carry him to bed.'

Mrs Blair, who had recovered her composure somewhat, immediately objected. 'Whose bed? He's not having my bed, nor George's.'

Sherlock Holmes affixed the lady with a terrifying glare under which Mrs Blair quailed. 'Well, sir,' she said defensively, 'it isn't proper. I can't have a man sharing my rooms even if George gives up his bed for him. It ain't right.'

'Correct,' said Holmes. 'I propose therefore, that both yourself and George spend the night at the Whitehart Hotel across the road at our expense, whilst Doctor Watson and myself remain here in your kitchen to watch over our man.'

Mrs Blair's whole mien underwent a complete change. She positively beamed at Holmes. 'Why, sir. That is an excellent suggestion. George, help Mr Holmes and Doctor Watson get this man into your bed.'

The night had grown old. Sherlock Holmes and I dozed fitfully in our fireside chairs. As for Tom Hockney, the morphine had done its work well, for on each occasion when I looked in on him he was sleeping soundly. In the kitchen Holmes stirred from his doze. 'How is the patient, old fellow?'

'He is resting comfortably.'

The kitchen range had burned low and I began to replenish the coal supply from the scuttle. Holmes jumped up and took down the teapot from the dresser. 'A little light refreshment, Doctor?' he asked as he seized the kettle which sat quietly singing on the hob.

'Thank you, Holmes.'

Whilst Holmes brewed the tea, I mused on the sequence of events which had brought Mr Hockney to seek succour at the door of Sherlock Holmes. Something else was also bothering me. How would our plans be affected by having a sick man on our hands?

Holmes was, it seemed, thinking along the same lines. 'You know, Watson,' he said as he handed me a steaming cup. 'I believe that fate in the shape of Mr Hockney has dealt us a trump card.'

'How's that?'

'Well, it seems to me that when I am supposed to be taken into the bosom of, what did you say was the name of the clinic?'

'The Pargetter Clinic.'

'Quite so, when I am supposed to be taken to the Pargetter Clinic, we will need a body. Mr Hockney will do very well.'

'Surely, Holmes, you cannot involve a sick man in our affairs?'

'You will agree Mr Hockney is in need of care and attention?'

'Undoubtedly, but...'

'Then where better for him to receive this attention than at an establishment which has been designed specifically for that very purpose?'

'What if he is visited by someone in high office.'

'You will ensure by the dire prognostications for my welfare contained in each new bulletin so that no one will desire to come into my presence?'

'What shall we tell Mr Hockney?'

'We shall tell him that he is receiving treatment fit for a king, because he is helping the forces of good outwit those of evil.'

I smiled. 'He can hardly refuse such a worthy task.'

At that moment a voice called out from

the bedroom. It was that of Tom Hockney. I ran to his bedside. The colour had returned to his face and his fever had passed.

'How do you feel?' I said.

'A great deal better, thank you, Doctor Watson,' he replied. 'Almost well enough to carry out the task I have heard you both so earnestly discussing.'

'How much have you overheard?'

The sailor smiled weakly. 'Enough to understand I am to be Mr Holmes's understudy while he goes off on some secret mission.'

The lean figure of Sherlock Holmes stood in the doorway, his wiry frame silhouetted by the light from the kitchen range. 'You will play the part, Mr Hockney?'

'Yes, sir. I will.'

'Capital, capital.'

Once again I attended to the needs of my patient. The bleeding had ceased. I changed the dressings and injected him with a little more morphine. Very soon he was sleeping once more.

It was much later when I awoke with a start; I was quite alone. Of Sherlock Holmes there was no sign. I glanced at the big clock above the dresser. Seven a.m.

There was a light but firm footfall in the passage and Holmes reappeared. 'Good morning, Watson.'

I rubbed the sleep from my eyes. Standing, I tried to stretch away the knots into which my muscles had turned during the night. 'Hello, Holmes. Have you looked in on our patient?'

'Indeed, he is awake and complaining of hunger pangs.'

'Excellent,' I said, reaching for my bag. 'I will examine him.' Mr Hockney was indeed feeling better. His recovery seemed ensured. Once more I changed his dressings, but on this occasion decided that a further injection of morphine was unnecessary.

When at last I returned to the kitchen, Holmes had made a fresh pot of tea and from somewhere he had unearthed a stockpot, from which he was making a little beef tea. 'Mr Hockney is recovering?' he said.

'Yes. He is improving rapidly.'

'Can he be moved?'

'Why yes, I believe so.'

'Then we must remove him from his bed downstairs and take him to our rooms. He may use my room. I have prepared the bed.'

'But why, Holmes?'

'Mrs Blair and son George will be

returning before long. I do not wish them to know that Mr Hockney is staying with us. They must believe he has been removed to another place of recovery during the night.'

It was fortunate that Holmes and I acted promptly. We had taken our patient upstairs in a chairlift and deposited him onto the bed in Holmes's room, when the key was turned in the lock of the front door. Looking down into the hallway I espied Mrs Blair.

'Good morning, Mrs Blair,' I cried. 'You are very early. It is not yet quite eight o'clock.'

The lady looked around her. 'Oh yes, Doctor Watson. I thought I might come back early to clear up.'

Behind me I heard the door of our sitting room open. Sherlock Holmes slipped silently onto the landing and handed me a note. It read:

Tell Mrs B that the patient has gone. Also inform her that Mr Holmes is unwell – a chill.

I looked at Holmes who merely smiled and waved me downstairs. I am not a good liar and dislike telling untruths, even in a good cause. Before I could speak, Mrs Blair provided the opportunity to begin in my deceptions.

'The man has gone, then?' she said.

'Yes. He was removed during the night.'

'Got worse, did he?'

'No. It was done just to be prudent.'

'Is Mr Holmes up and about?'

'No. During the night he also began to feel a little unwell.'

'Oh. Nothing serious I hope?'

'A chill.'

Although it was quite clear that Mrs Blair could have no inkling of the subterfuge being played upon her, her innocent questions seemed to be planned to catch me out.

Mrs Blair looked closely at me. 'You don't look so good yourself, Doctor Watson.'

I laughed. 'It is nothing. Just a lack of sleep.'

'Well. When I've tidied up a bit I'll bring you up some breakfast. Will Mr Holmes require anything?'

'Perhaps a little beef tea, Mrs Blair.'

'Then you go back to him. I'll be up directly.'

During my absence Sherlock Holmes had built up a good fire in our sitting room. He had acquired a rug and had slipped into his dressing gown.

After a delay of twenty minutes or so, a light footfall was to be heard on the stairs.

'Mrs Blair,' remarked Holmes.

'Come right in,' I cried.

Mrs Blair entered with a tray piled quite high with provender. 'Your breakfast, Doctor Watson,' she said her eyes dancing around the sitting room. 'Oh, Mr Holmes, you do look poorly.'

Sherlock Holmes smiled weakly from within the confines of his blanket. 'Thank you, dear lady. Just leave my cup on the table. I will take some nourishment presently.'

No sooner had the lady departed when Holmes leaped from his chair and began inspecting the breakfast tray. 'This is excellent, Watson. Kidneys, bacon, eggs and toast – fortunately there is enough for two.' He sat down at the table. 'Come along, Doctor, or there will be none for you.'

After breakfast Sherlock Holmes and I sat talking once more with Tom Hockney. Holmes was keen to extract every ounce of information about the sequence of events which brought the mariner to our doorstep. 'Mr Hockney. You say that three men came on board your ship. Are you able to describe them?'

'Yes, sir. Two of them, the kidnappers, were dressed in long black coats. They were both big men. One was fair with a large moustache, the other was dark and clean shaven. Both were about five and thirty.'

'And the third man?' said Holmes making careful notes.

'He was quite different. Just a little taller than myself, he was. Some would describe him as quite good looking. He was dressed in an old brown coat, which was much too big for him.' The sailor closed his eyes as if attempting to create a mental picture of the man he was describing. 'Yes,' he said quite suddenly. 'He was wearing a waistcoat, but no jacket.'

Holmes looked keenly at the sailor. 'His face, Mr Hockney. Do you remember his face?'

'Ah. I do, sir, but there was something much more striking than his face by which I'll remember him. His eyes – black as coal they were. Gypsy eyes, or I'm a Dutchman.'

Sherlock Holmes and I looked at each other and exclaimed in unison. 'Hunter Andrews.'

Tom Hockney looked first at Sherlock Holmes and then at myself. He was clearly astonished. 'You know this man?'

'He is presently at the centre of a case which is currently baffling Scotland Yard,' said Holmes crisply.

'At what time does your ship sail, Mr Hockney?' I asked.

The sailor gave the matter a little thought. 'She was due to sail on the midnight tide tonight. But as the kidnapping was observed by myself, the captain may have taken her out last night.'

'Then the police may be too late if they are sent,' said Holmes thoughtfully.

'Will the ship have any port of call other than Naples?' I queried.

'No, Doctor Watson. Naples is her only destination.'

'But of course the captain may have secret plans to dock elsewhere,' said Holmes.

I sighed. 'And, we cannot be certain if he would even dock. He could merely send a rowing boat ashore.'

'Things do not look good for Mr Andrews.'

'At any rate, we should inform Mrs Andrews of her husband's fate.'

'Indeed.'

After ensuring the continuing comfort of my patient and seeing that his wounds were clean, I joined Sherlock Holmes in our sitting room. His brow was clouded in thought. 'It seems to me, my dear fellow, that whilst my supposed illness has enabled me to drop out of sight, it has also prevented me from a continuing investigation of the kidnapping of Mr Hunter Andrews.'

'I suppose that on this occasion the greater need must supersede the lesser,' I mused.

'But to Mrs Andrews the disappearance and possible death of her husband represent the greater need. I must do for her what I can.'

'Is there much you can do?'

Holmes thought for a long moment. Then a brief smile played across his face. 'Watson, I will continue the investigation in disguise.'

Immediately, Holmes retired to his dressing room. A few minutes later the door reopened and the figure of an elderly cleric stepped out. The old man fingered his long white hair and peered myopically at me through half-moon spectacles. He leaned heavily on a silver-tipped cane, his ancient legs barely carrying him across the room.

'Wonderful,' I cried. 'A total metamorphosis.'

'You have remembered me?' said the cleric in a wheezy voice.

'Indeed. I have twice met you before. As I recall both meetings were on memorable occasions – when you encountered Irene Adler and when we were fleeing the intrigues of Moriarty,' I laughed. 'The stage has lost a fine actor, Holmes.'

'Why thank you, Doctor,' said Holmes, regaining his usual height and posture. 'Now, when I am gone you will write a note for Chief Inspector Lestrade citing the information about Mr Andrews which has come to hand. You must not, however, disclose the source. Mr Hockney must be allowed to remain free of Scotland Yard.'

'And what if Lestrade desires a personal interview?'

Holmes laughed. 'Lestrade will gain nothing from any interview and I believe he will not desire to return again to this address in a hurry.'

'What if he desires to meet Mr Hockney at Scotland Yard?'

Sherlock Holmes took up his stick and once more became an elderly cleric. 'God be with you, my son,' he said. Then he was gone, leaving me to ponder on my unanswered question.

The afternoon had grown old when Sherlock Holmes returned. For some time I had been dozing before the fire. The note I had sent around to Scotland Yard had as yet elicited no response and when I heard the doorbell I half expected my visitor to be a policeman responding to my information, but it was Holmes himself. He looked rather pleased with himself.

'Brr. It is a cold day,' he remarked as he briskly rubbed his hands together in front of the fire. 'You have received no reply from the police?'

'Nothing.'

'We must hope that they have acted on the information.'

As Holmes discarded his make-up he proceeded to enlighten me about his visit to Mrs Andrews. 'You may imagine the look of surprise on the face of the lady when she saw an elderly clergyman on her doorstep,' he chuckled. 'At first I could see that she was tempted to send me away. When I informed her of my connection with Sherlock Holmes and Doctor Watson, she relented and invited me in for some tea.'

'Did you reveal your true nature?' I said.

'I did not. You may think me foolish, Watson, but I thought it better that bad news would come better from the lips of a clergyman.'

'And Mrs Andrews, was she much upset by the news?'

'Indeed. The poor young woman.'

I was much taken by this new side of Sherlock Holmes. Hitherto, womenkind had been the target of scorn, insincere charm, or apathy. But pity was an emotion wholly new to him.

'Holmes, you surprise me,' I said.

'The loss of a loved one will open the deepest and most hurtful wounds, Doctor. This much I have recently discovered,' he said severely.

Holmes threw himself into his chair and gratefully eased his feet from the confines of his clerical shoes. 'There arose two items of information which made my visit more successful, however,' he said. 'When I described to Mrs Andrews the two men seen by Mr Hockney, escorting her husband, she was immediately able to identify them.

'"Why, Mr Holding," she said. That was the name by which I introduced myself. "Those descriptions closely resemble those of two of Hunter's sometime associates. The blond man could be Mr Wilson and the dark man must surely be Mr Turner."

'When I asked Mrs Andrews for how long her husband had done business with these gentlemen she told me that some six months before Mr Wilson had engaged him to open his safe, which had unaccountably become jammed shut. It was at the same office he had also first met Mr Turner. She never knew their forenames. Mrs Andrews told me that her husband had done various tasks in their employ. Indeed, they had recommended him to several of their business associates.

'When I enquired about the nature of these men, Mrs Andrews said that although she had on several occasions observed them at a distance she had never actually met them in person.

'"Mr Andrews found them a little odd," she said.

'When I enquired in which way did he find them odd, he had told her that, for example, although they bore English names, they were clearly foreigners.'

'That is not so uncommon, Holmes,' I said. 'Over the last eighty years many foreigners have become domiciled here and have Anglicized their names.'

'Indeed. It was, however, something to build upon. A piece of evidence which could possibly provide the key to the mystery. I asked Mrs Andrews if she could provide the business address of Messrs Turner and Wilson. Fortunately, Mr Andrews was meticulous about such matters and upon examining an index I was able to discover that the address was in Bow.'

'You continued your investigations in Bow?'

'Exactly. The address to which I was directed is a large four-storey building off Bromley-by-Bow. The offices I required were on the top floor.'

'They were empty, of course.'

'You are perceptive, Watson. When I spoke to the man in the offices down the corridor he told me that the two gentlemen had packed up and gone two days before. When I enquired if they had left any forwarding address, to where do you suppose they had informed him they were going?'

'To Italy,' I hazarded.

'To Russia,' said Holmes drily.

'Good grief.'

'I asked this gentleman if it were possible to view the offices, as they might be exactly the premises I needed for my evangelical work. He said yes. The men had left the key with him and the landlord had not yet collected it, but as he was presently engaged in some pressing business of his own, would I mind seeing them alone?'

Sherlock Holmes drew on his dressing gown and reached for his pipe and the Persian slipper in which his tobacco was kept. 'There were two large rooms in the suite. Both had been left as if the occupants were expected to immediately return. The first room had been exclusively used as an office. There was the usual apparel associated with a business, desks, cabinets and so on. It was the other room, however, which interested me.

'The office had been converted into a bed-sitting room. Two single beds lined the walls and there was a sofa, an armchair and deal table with two upright chairs. In one corner was a large spirit stove, which had doubtless provided cooking facilities for the men.

'Imagine my excitation when I discovered that the room had been occupied not by two men, but by three.'

'Hunter Andrews,' I exclaimed.

'It could be none other,' said Holmes crisply.

'You were able to glean sufficient evidence from the room to be certain?'

'I espied sufficient evidence to indicate the presence of a third person, who had been held captive. That third person was un-doubtedly Mr Andrews.'

Sherlock Holmes lay back in his chair, puffing contemplatively on his pipe.

'Holmes?'

'Yes, my dear fellow?'

'Can it be possible that Mr Andrews has indeed been spirited away to Russia?'

'Indeed. It is possible. We know at least that he is being taken to Italy as indicated by Mr Hockney's observations.'

'They could be taking him by another route, by way of the Baltic or even Archangel.'

Holmes leaned forward and lit a spill from the fire. 'I think not, Watson. Certainly the Baltic ports are iced up at this time of the year. As for Archangel, an old tramp steamer would simply not be robust enough to survive such a rough voyage. I believe that the ship will sail for Italy as planned.'

'But Mr Andrews could be taken off in France and the journey continue overland.'

Sherlock Holmes relit his pipe and blew out the spill. 'You are not thinking, Watson. An unwilling prisoner would best be kept away from possible public gaze. If he were to be carried overland, Mr Andrews might cry out for assistance; perhaps he would attempt to escape. If, however, he was taken by ship, his cries would go unheeded and to where would he escape?'

'Then had we not better contact the harbour master at Ramsgate in order to discover if the *Pride of Thanet* has sailed?' I cried.

'It is done,' said Holmes. 'The telegraph office was my first port of call. If you will excuse the pun.'

'Then you have also sent a telegram to his counterpart at Naples?'

'Of course, Watson, in the name of the Metropolitan Police, I warned him that the *Pride of Thanet* was suspected of carrying a victim of kidnapping and that he should have the ship inspected as soon as she docks.'

'Well done, Holmes.'

'Thank you, Watson. I have done as much as I am able to assist the Andrews family. Now I must turn my attentions to the Holmes family.' He stretched out his legs. 'You will prepare Mr Hockney for a journey, Watson, for tomorrow we leave for Sussex.'

FOUR

When the morning broke it proved to be cold, clammy and cheerless. A steady drizzle filled the skies and slowly saturated the streets.

Sherlock Holmes was up and about before it was light. His packing was completed and he sat moodily before the fire, awaiting the hour of our departure.

I rose at seven-thirty and had barely washed and shaved before Holmes was at my door. 'Watson. At this very moment a telegram boy is about to deliver some expected replies to yesterday's messages. Be a good fellow and collect them for me.'

The doorbell clanged. I knotted my tie and pulled on my jacket. As I reached the front door, Mrs Blair came out of her kitchen. She was holding a newspaper, which she waved in my face. 'This is really too bad!' she cried. 'Having a madman in this house. It is too bad.'

Very much surprised at her mien, I enquired from the lady the meaning of her outburst.

'This is what I mean,' she exclaimed, shoving the newspaper into my hand and tapping at it with an agitated forefinger.

I scanned the article which ran:

MR SHERLOCK HOLMES
TAKEN ILL
Severe mental problems, says 'friend'

Today we can reveal the sad tale of the decline into mental illness of one of England's greatest minds. Mr Sherlock Holmes, the well known detective, for some years retired to Sussex, has returned to his old haunts at 221B Baker Street to consult his colleague and friend Doctor John Watson, whom we understand, has confirmed the diagnosis.

A close friend of Mr Holmes tells us that he is often to be seen frothing at the mouth and crawling around on all fours. It is the sad decline into the dark world of madness which leads his friend to concern himself for the safety of all those with whom Mr Holmes comes into contact. Further reports of this matter will be printed in this newspaper as they come to hand.

'Well?' demanded Mrs Blair. 'What do you have to say?' She snatched the newspaper back and once more began to read the lurid report. 'To think that only yesterday I was speaking with him in my own kitchen.'

I bent down and picked up the telegrams, which the boy had deposited on the mat. 'The report is a gross exaggeration, Mrs Blair,' I said, 'but perhaps you will be happy in your mind to know that Mr Holmes and myself are today returning to Sussex where at least he will receive a warm welcome.'

I had hardly put a foot on the bottom step when there came a further ring at the bell. I opened the door to find I was in the presence of General Wilton.

'Hello, John. This is a bloody business indeed,' he said. 'Is Mr Holmes truly as bad as the newspapers say?'

I led the general upstairs to our rooms. Holmes who had clearly heard all that had gone before sat wrapped in a blanket by the fire.

'How are you, Mr Holmes?' said our visitor.

'I am as well as can be expected.'

The general sat down on the sofa. He looked troubled. 'John, I must confess that when last I saw you both, it concerned me greatly that Mr Holmes might be the victim of something more than temporary hysteria. It was I who instructed Chief Inspector Lestrade to come and investigate. When Lestrade reported that Mr Holmes had become mad, my worst fears were confirmed. My dear fellow, he must have treatment.'

I patted the old soldier on the arm. 'Do not concern yourself, Jimmy. Mr Holmes will receive the very best of care. Today he is returning home to Sussex and in two days' time he will be admitted to the Pargetter Clinic in Newhaven.'

'But how long will it before Mr Holmes recovers?'

'It will be at least three months, perhaps longer.'

The general bowed his head. 'You will return to Baker Street afterwards?'

'No. I shall stay with Holmes for as long as he needs me.'

General Wilton stood up again. 'Will you require a travelling companion?'

'Thank you, no,' I replied. 'We are being accompanied by an old friend, a minister whom we have both known for many years.'

'Very well. I trust that you will both have a safe journey and that you, Mr Holmes, will be better very soon,' said the general, warmly shaking me by the hand.

'Goodbye, General,' said Holmes weakly.

'Thank you, Jimmy,' I said quietly, as I watched the old soldier make his exit.

At once Holmes sprang out of his chair. His eyes were blazing, his face was flushed. 'Humbug!' he cried.

'Really, Holmes,' I said. 'You are unfair.'

Holmes snorted. 'Watson. Do you think that after forty years of judging people, I can now be so easily taken in by a palpable liar?'

The vehemence of Sherlock Holmes forced me to modify my objection. 'Possibly, perhaps the general does not, for himself, care one way or another, but perhaps he is following the instructions of one who does.'

Holmes sighed. 'Well, possibly. But it does not matter a great deal. He will tell his master about my present affliction, which is all that matters.' He threw off the blanket and stretched himself to his full height. 'Now tell me, Watson, what was the nature of your heated conversation with the excellent Mrs Blair?'

It was whilst I was explaining to Holmes the content of my conversation, that I remembered the telegrams so carelessly stuffed into my pocket.

'Ah,' said Holmes eagerly, rubbing his long thin hands together. 'At last.'

He tore open the envelopes and devoured the contents. 'It is as I expected, Watson. The *Pride of Thanet* did indeed sail a day early. But I foresee vexation and misfortune awaiting them in Italy, where the harbour-master informs you that he had the very same day received a request from Scotland Yard to search the ship.'

'Excellent,' I cried. 'Perhaps before long Mr Andrews will be home safely.'

'Indeed.'

The train squeaked and rattled its way out of London Bridge Station, bound for Newhaven and the villa belonging to Sherlock Holmes, high on the Sussex downs.

I had engaged a compartment for my two travelling companions, Sherlock Holmes, Tom Hockney and myself. We looked an ill-assorted bunch. Holmes disguised as an elderly nonconformist minister, Mr Hockney wrapped in a heavy coat, deerstalker hat and several scarves, for all the world the very image of Sherlock Holmes; and myself, disguised as no one but Doctor John H. Watson, MD (retired).

As I sat watching the grey smoky streets of south London slip by, I ruminated on the events which had brought my companions and myself to the point where two of us were in heavy disguise and the other, after leading a life of the strictest rectitude, had been the purveyor of numerous untruths and deceptions. Surely upon the day of atonement when we have to explain our sins, the punishment meted out in my case would be of the severest nature.

Sherlock Holmes reached out and tugged at my sleeve. 'A penny for your thoughts, my dear fellow.'

'Oh,' I said morosely, 'I was just cogitating on the number of deceptions in which I have recently assisted.'

Holmes laughed heartily. 'You should have been me for the last thirty-five years, Watson. Then you might have something to worry about.'

The journey to Newhaven was relatively uneventful. Mr Hockney, however, found the expedition a tiring matter, but he found himself unable to sleep. I accordingly injected him with a little dilute morphine.

The train began to slow. We had almost reached our destination. Holmes stood up and pulled his bag from the rack.

The train rumbled into the precincts of Newhaven. I gave Tom Hockney a gentle shake. 'Tom, we are nearly in the station.'

For a moment he looked a little dazed. Then he smiled and nodded. I turned to assist Holmes with the bags. Then the most extraordinary thing happened. Tom was on his feet pointing with a shaky hand towards the platform. 'The man! The man!' he cried.

'Which man?' I said, thinking Tom still to be under the influence of the narcotic I had earlier administered to him.

'The man who attacked me. Look there.

The large bearded man at the barrier.'

Holmes placed a solicitous hand on the shoulder of the agitated seaman. 'Do not concern yourself, Tom. You are quite out of danger. He will not recognize you.'

Holmes slid open the compartment's door and peered into the corridor. 'Watson. Directly the train stops, I shall alight and make my way to the barrier, where I will remain in the vicinity. You will retrieve the bath chair from the guard's van and assist Mr Hockney. The fellow may recognize Doctor Watson and if he does he will most assuredly assume that your companion is Holmes. I will create a diversion which will ensure that you will not be molested,' Holmes chuckled. 'No one will suspect the actions of an elderly non-conformist clergyman.'

'What then are we to do, Holmes?' I said.

'A carriage has been ordered to take us to Cliff House. If for any reason I have not joined you within ten minutes you will tell the driver to leave without me. I will come as soon as maybe.'

Without another word Sherlock Holmes stepped down from the carriage and quickly became lost in the throng. A few moments later he reappeared at the barrier.

Tom Hockney grabbed my sleeve. 'Doctor

Watson, Mr Holmes has fallen, will he be all right?'

I smiled. Holmes had fallen at the very feet of the large bearded man. 'I believe that Mr Holmes will be just fine.'

A few moments later Tom and I were safely ensconced in our carriage. Then, from the alleyway, which led from the station exit there came the voice of Holmes. 'Thank you, sir. You need trouble yourself no longer. Here is my conveyance. My friends, Mr Holmes and Doctor Watson, with whom I am staying for a few days, will assist me now.'

I listened with a growing sense of alarm as he continued. 'Did I tell you, sir, that Mr Holmes is presently very unwell. Indeed he is an invalid. Although I am, myself, not in the best of health, I have travelled down to stay with Mr Holmes at his cliff-top house near Fulworth, to give him the spiritual succour he so desperately requires during his convalescence... Ah, here we are. Thank you, sir. God be with you.'

'Holmes,' I hissed between clenched teeth. 'What on earth are you doing?'

Sherlock Holmes held up his hand. 'Please, Doctor. This is neither the time nor is it the place. Drive on, cabby.'

The carriage lurched forwards and

moments later we had turned onto the Fulworth road. Holmes looked at our startled expressions and burst out laughing. Tom and I looked at each other in surprise. Unable to contain myself I spoke sharply. 'Holmes. We have just heard you well nigh issue that fellow an invitation to come calling. Sooner or later he, and I imagine several of his cronies, will arrive, possibly at dead of night, determined to discover what exactly we know about the kidnapping of Hunter Andrews.'

'Exactly, my dear fellow. I have laid a trail which he cannot fail to follow.'

'It was a deliberate ploy?'

'Indeed. Our friend would sooner or later have discovered our movements. He would have come for us eventually. Now it is certain he will come quickly. When he does, we will be waiting for him.'

It was my turn to laugh. 'It will be a complete turning of the tables. We shall be able to discover exactly what he knows. Holmes, you are a genius.'

Holmes bowed his head in recognition of my praise. 'Possibly, Doctor. Possibly,' he said.

Mrs Oliver was pleased to see us. 'Why, Mr

Holmes, Doctor Watson. Come right in. Welcome, Reverend. I have just made some tea.' The good lady placed her hand on the arm of the muffled figure in the bath chair. 'Are you feeling any better, Mr Holmes? The papers were full of such lurid reports about your illness.'

'Thank you, Mrs Oliver. I am quite well.'

The housekeeper gave a start as she heard the well-known tones of Sherlock Holmes emanating from the person of an elderly minister. 'Oh, Mr Holmes. You gave me quite a turn. Why are you all dressed up? Then who is this gentleman?'

Sherlock Holmes briefly explained the situation, taking the housekeeper into his confidence without demur.

Mrs Oliver turned to me with a glint in her eyes. 'I suppose it really is you, Doctor Watson?'

I laughed. 'Rest assured, Mrs Oliver. It is I.'

In the kitchen Holmes pounced upon an envelope. Briefly he scanned the script and held it out to me.

'It is a note from Jacks,' I said. 'Arrangements have been completed. A carriage will call for us at eight a.m. tomorrow.'

'Excellent.'

After supper, Mrs Oliver took her leave

and, when Tom was safely ensconced in his bed, Sherlock Holmes and I settled down by the kitchen range. A warm glow seemed to spread around the room. Holmes took a taper from the fire and lit his pipe, whilst I enjoyed a cigar.

'The calm before the storm, Holmes?' I ventured.

Holmes smiled. 'Indeed old fellow.' He took out his watch and looked at it. 'It is now ten-thirty. We should have a few more hours of solitude.'

'You have laid your plans?'

'Our visitors will enjoy a rousing reception.'

The warmth of the kitchen allied to the tiredness, which the journey had induced, quickly lulled me into a fitful slumber. Dreams of sailors and madmen, policemen and doctors, and kings and poisoners stirred my serenity.

I awoke with a start. Sherlock Holmes was standing over me. 'Watson. The hour has come. I have seen lights on the road. A car has stopped at the top of the steps.'

I struggled to my feet. In the dim light of the declining fire, I could see the glint in his eyes. 'Tom is securely locked away?' I asked.

'He will be quite safe.'

'Very well. Tell me, what should I do?'

'All doors and windows, with the exception of the rear scullery door, are locked and bolted. Our visitors will find an easy access. You will await them at this door. It allows an excellent view of the egress. You have your service revolver with you?'

I nodded.

'Excellent. When they enter, you will hold them up. If they are armed the heavy door will afford excellent protection.

I took a deep breath. 'You will not be here with me, Holmes?'

'I am about to slip out. With any luck I shall be able to surprise them from the rear.'

He made to go out into the night, then turned once more to face me. 'Be bold, my dear Watson. We have faced mightier foes and have been in tighter corners.'

Then he was gone into the blackness of the night. Holmes was scarcely out of sight when I detected muffled footsteps. At any moment a figure would appear at the scullery door. Holmes was correct. My position afforded me an excellent view yet it rendered me safe cover.

A window nearby to the path was rattled, then the front door was tried. It would be just a matter of moments before the back door was reached.

There was a noise behind me. My heart leaped into my mouth; someone was at the kitchen window. I thanked Holmes for having the foresight to draw the curtains.

Then at last after what, to my taut nerves, seemed hours, but I supposed could have been only five minutes, the scullery door opened. A face peered into the room. In the half light, I could see that it was the large bearded man. Cautiously he pushed the door open a little more. He whispered something under his breath to an invisible companion. Then the door was swung open and the bearded man and his companion, a tall, blond man in his early thirties, entered silently.

'Do not close the door,' said the other man sharply. 'We do not need a barrier to our exit.'

'Well, we are in,' said the bearded man. 'What now?'

His companion pulled out a large, ugly-looking cosh and slapped it into the palm of his left hand. 'We shall ask Mr Holmes and Doctor Watson a few questions. That is all.'

'I don't like it. What if they cry out?'

'What if they do? Who shall hear them?'

'I still don't like it.'

'You will do as you are told.'

There was no doubt in my mind what our fate would have been should we have fallen into the hands of these villains. My anger overcame my fears and I stood full in the doorway, revolver in my hand. 'Stand still!' I cried. 'If you do not obey, I shall shoot you down.'

'Gripes!' ejaculated the bearded man.

His companion made to advance. Then, seeing my resolve, thought better of it. He smiled and spread his hands out before him. 'Please do not shoot,' he said in a most ingratiating manner. 'We have not come to harm you.'

'Then, why are you prowling about at the dead of night?' I demanded. 'Why do you come calling at an hour when decent folk are in bed and asleep?'

He shrugged and looked rueful. 'Ah well. You are right. But perhaps we may come to some arrangement? Maybe we can get the answers to our questions and no harm done?'

It was my turn to smile. 'I think not. I believe it will be yourself answering *our* questions.'

'Questions to which I hope you will have excellent answers,' said Sherlock Holmes from the open doorway behind our visitors.

'Sherlock Holmes?' said the blond man, in

a voice that betrayed both shock and disbelief.

'Indeed.'

Holmes moved slowly towards the centre of the room keeping our adversaries covered at all times. The bearded man surveyed us with frightened eyes. 'Now 'ere, Mr Holmes,' he said. 'You don't want to do nothing hasty. Mr Wilson here only wants to know the answers to some questions. We don't mean you no harm.'

Holmes threw back his head and laughed loudly. 'My dear, sir. I am not so foolish to believe that.'

Suddenly Wilson gave the bearded man a heavy shove into the path of Sherlock Holmes. There was a loud bang as Holmes's gun went off. The man gave a cry and slumped to the floor.

Using the momentary confusion to cover his attempt to escape Wilson pushed past Holmes and threw open the door.

'Watson!' cried Holmes. 'Stop him!'

I fired my revolver but missed, the bullet thudding into the heavy oak door. As quickly as I was able, I ran to the exit. Outside I could hear running footsteps in the darkness. Twice more I fired my revolver in the direction of the escaping villain, more in hope than in expectation of actually hitting him. Realizing there was little more I could do about the escaping felon, I returned to the scullery, the door still open, the light streaming out into the night. As I reached the door, there came the distant sound of a car roaring into life. Wilson, I realized, had escaped.

'Watson, is that you?' It was the voice of Sherlock Holmes.

'Yes, my dear fellow. I am here.'

'Come quickly. I am in need of your medical expertise.'

I found Holmes kneeling beside the prone body of the bearded man. He had placed a folded coat beneath the man's head and was pressing firmly on his chest with a large towel. The towel was stained red. The man was clearly bleeding heavily. A quick glance was sufficient for me to observe that the poor fellow was not long for this world. I communicated the fact to Holmes, with a quick shake of the head. Holmes pulled a face of disappointment. 'A pity, Watson. A pity.'

The man stirred and opened his eyes. 'You've done for me, Mr Holmes.'

Holmes took the man's head gently in his hands. 'What is your name, my man?' he said.

'Parker, Vincent Parker.'

'Why did you come here tonight, Mr Parker?'

'Holmes,' I said sharply.

Ignoring my admonishment, Holmes continued his questioning of the dying man. 'You came here at the request of Mr Wilson, did you not?'

'Yes, sir,' said the man weakly. 'We came here to find out if you knew about the kidnapping.'

'You also assaulted Mr Hockney, did you not?'

The man nodded. He began to cough violently. Holmes looked at me. 'Is there something you can do for this poor fellow, Watson?'

'I have a little morphine which may ease his pain a little, but more I cannot do.'

Parker looked at us with dark, intense eyes. 'May I have a drink? My mouth is so dry.'

I turned to the pump and drew a little water, but as I turned back again Parker gave a sigh and expired. Holmes stood up again. He looked particularly grim. 'This is a bad business, Watson.'

I nodded. 'Yes. But you cannot blame yourself for Parker's death. It was Wilson shoving him into you, which caused your revolver to go off. Wilson is the culprit, Holmes.'

Holmes pulled the coat out from under the dead man's head and draped it across the body. 'I think, however, the forces of law and order would not see things quite that way.'

'What on earth do you mean?'

'Place yourself in the shoes of the local sergeant, Watson. You have been informed by a friend of Mr Holmes that Mr Holmes has just accidentally shot an intruder.'

'Well. What of it?'

Holmes smiled and gently patted my arm, 'Just this, my dear fellow. You have been informed that it was Mr Holmes, who has very recently been featured in every newspaper in the land as a lunatic. Would you not at the very least have Holmes securely locked away until the matter was carefully investigated?'

Holmes, of course, was exactly right. Any policeman worth his salt would insist that someone with Holmes's present reputation would be closely questioned even with a friend's testimony to the effect that it was an accident.

'Possibly they would not hold you in custody, Holmes. My testimony might allow you your freedom.'

'And in the meantime we would be held here against our will. It would amount to the same thing.'

'Then what are we to do?'

'We will handle the matter ourselves, Watson. The police cannot be involved. Our time is too precious.'

'But what are we to do with Parker?'

'We will have to dispose of the late Mr Parker in such a way that when the corpse eventually comes to light there will be no taint of suspicion on ourselves.'

'But how are we to do that?'

'We shall have to bury him in the sea.'

For a moment my senses reeled. My breath was quite literally taken away by the suggestion Holmes had laid before me. 'Surely, Holmes. You cannot be serious? It is so ... un-christian.'

'The man is dead, nothing we do can harm him further. The life of my brother and the peace of Europe may hang upon our actions tonight.' Holmes grabbed me by both wrists and looked deeply and earnestly into my eyes. 'Watson, we have to do it.'

Holmes, of course, was right. Still, it was a terrible and grisly business. The only comfort I could derive from our actions was the fact that Parker had stabbed and very nearly killed Tom Hockney, and would in all probability have allowed Wilson to shoot Holmes and myself like dogs. It was, however, a task which we carried out with heavy hearts.

Sherlock Holmes had found an old tarpaulin in one of the outhouses and he wrapped it around the body. We carried it down the steps to the cliff edge and laid it on the grass. Holmes slid the glass back on the lantern, revealing his face, white and pinched in the cold night air, his hair flying in the strong wind.

'You said a little earlier that throwing Parker over the cliff edge was un-christian, Watson. Perhaps you are right. Can you think of it as a burial at sea? If you have a few appropriate words to say perhaps your conscience will be somewhat salved.'

I cannot be sure if it was the distress and remorse in my heart, or merely the stinging wind, which brought the tears to my eyes. Perhaps it was a little of both. A short prayer, which I shall forever remember, came to my mind. 'By the grace of God, we commit the body of Vincent Parker, a grievous sinner, into the arms of the deep. May the Lord have mercy upon his soul.'

Holmes pulled one string and I pulled the other and the body of Vincent Parker disappeared over the cliff edge into the boiling sea, a hundred feet below.

The night of 13th/14th March 1912 is one I shall never forget. Holmes was expecting Mrs Oliver at seven and there was much that needed to be done to remove all evidence of the presence of Vincent Parker. The scullery floor had to be washed clean of his blood and the linen soiled by his blood had to be burned in the kitchen range. The tarpaulin which had been wrapped around the body needed to be thoroughly washed and returned to its place of origin. It was a little before six a.m. when finally we fell into our beds.

Sleep was simply impossible and Mrs Oliver was soon to be heard bustling about downstairs. Before long she was knocking on my door with my morning tea. 'Goodness me, Doctor Watson. You look as if you've been up all night.'

I smiled wanly at the housekeeper. 'It seems as much to me, Mrs Oliver.'

'That's too bad, with such a busy day in front of you,' she said, as she placed the tray on my bedside cabinet. 'I expect it was the excitement of your little venture what's kept you awake?'

'Yes, Mrs Oliver,' I said wearily. 'It was the excitement, right enough.'

At breakfast, Holmes seemed just as usual. I envied him his powers of recovery. Tom had joined us and was consuming a large plate of porridge.

Mrs Oliver opened a jar of honey, one of the fruits of Holmes's lifestyle in Sussex. Tom took a spoon and helped himself to a generous portion. 'Doctor Watson, was there any thunder during the night?'

'Thunder? No. I believe it was a clear night, Tom. Why do you ask?'

'Well, sir. It must have been during the early hours. I heard some banging. I took it to be thunder and went back to sleep.'

For a second, I thought Holmes would jump out of his chair. As it was, he spilled his coffee. Mrs Oliver took a tea towel and quickly wiped the table. 'Careful now, Mr Holmes. You haven't spilled any on yourself, have you?'

Tom Hockney looked at Holmes and then at myself. In his bright eyes I thought I espied a glimmer of understanding. 'Ah well, I must have dreamed it then,' he said.

The hospital vehicle arrived promptly at eight a.m. Holmes once more faced the world as a non-conformist clergyman, whilst Tom Hockney was again wrapped in a blanket and felt hat. Mrs Oliver stood in the doorway and bade us farewell. 'Goodbye, Mr Holmes, Doctor Watson. The very best of luck go with you on your long journey. To-night and every night I will light a candle and place it in the garret awaiting your safe return.'

As the carriage rattled along the road to Newhaven I fell into a brown study. Over the years Sherlock Holmes and I had been in many a tight corner and had taken part in some unlawful pursuits, but we had never become involved in such a dreadful business as the death and disposal of Vincent Parker. Indeed, during the recent few days, I had lied, cheated, misled or allowed others to mislead themselves and now had been instrumental in the concealment of a serious matter. I was not proud of Doctor Watson. I could only comfort myself in some small measure by thinking of the future and the positive good we were about to do.

Holmes tapped me on the shoulder. 'A penny for your thoughts, old man.'

'I was just thinking, Holmes. Does heaven accept those who lie and cheat, even when it is in a good cause?'

Holmes laughed. 'Possibly not, Watson. I do however think that you are a little premature in your thoughts. Ask me again in twenty years or so when we have grown old and have maybe earned a few indulgences from mother church.'

It was towards ten a.m. when we arrived at the gates of the Pargetter Clinic. Doctor Morrison, the consultant physician, was waiting at the main entrance for us. Jacks had arranged everything beautifully. Tom Hockney was settled into a private room at the back of the clinic. He was admitted under the name of Sherlock Holmes and he was assigned to the care of myself, who, as far as the world was concerned, would be personally supervising his rest and recuperation.

I handed Morrison a sheaf of papers I had been carrying. Each paper was a bulletin describing the supposed progress of Sherlock Holmes. My instructions were that a fresh disclosure should be made on a weekly basis. If, however, we had not returned to England after six weeks, the doctor would have to issue bulletins, as he thought fit.

After lunch we bade farewell to Tom Hockney. The sailor was comfortably ensconced in his bed. Everything he required was positioned conveniently to hand. 'Well, Tom,' I said with much feeling. 'We are leaving now and I for one would like to express my thanks to you for your cooperation in this very delicate matter.'

I shook him warmly by the hand. Sherlock Holmes did likewise.

'I sincerely hope you find your brother safe and well, Mr Holmes,' said Tom.

'Thanks to you, my dear fellow, I believe that I shall.'

We turned to leave, but Tom called us back to his bedside. He beckoned us closer and spoke in little more than a whisper. 'Incidentally, Doctor Watson. I hope you hit that fellow you were shooting at last night. Thunder indeed.' He laughed wheezily. 'Good day, gentlemen.'

Holmes led the way down the corridor to the consultant physician's office. Just as we turned into the waiting room he stopped me. 'I believe, Watson, that not all gentlemen wear frock coats and speak with middle-class accents. Some are horny handed-seamen, roughly dressed and inelegantly spoken.'

Doctor Morrison's office was empty of human existence, but hanging from the hat stand was a suit of clothes I recognized as being my own. Jacks had thoughtfully sent on my blue serge along with my black boots freshly soled and heeled. On a small side table stood a ewer of hot water, a bowl and a neatly folded towel. Holmes picked up the towel and handed it to me. I unfolded it and discovered a stick of shaving soap and a safety razor.

'For me?' I said, puzzled. 'If you remember, Holmes, I have already shaved today.'

'Indeed, my dear fellow. You have, however, not shaved your entire face.'

'What do you mean, Holmes?'

'I mean your moustache.'

'You cannot wish me to shave off my moustache, Holmes? I have not shaved my upper lip for over thirty-five years.'

'Yes, and I am sorry to have to ask you to do so now, Watson.'

'But why?'

'You will agree, will you not, Doctor, that when the nonconformist clergyman leaves the clinic he should not do so in the company of anyone resembling Doctor Watson?'

'Yes, but...'

'You will recall, Doctor Watson is staying on at the clinic to tend to Mr Holmes. He therefore cannot be in two places at once, both on the loose with the minister, and issuing bulletins concerning the health of the patient he so assiduously attends.' Holmes prodded me with a bony forefinger. 'It therefore necessitates the need for the person seen leaving the clinic with me to be as differently attired as possible from Doctor Watson.'

I sighed. After all the terrible things I had been through so recently, the loss of a moustache should have been small beer indeed. It was, however, a moment when I finally observed in the mirror this rather sad-looking man with the curiously pink top lip, staring back at me. My disguise was further heightened by the wearing of a pair of gold-framed glasses, fortunately fitted with plain glass. With these changes, I cannot say that I felt myself to be a new man, although I certainly looked a different one, going into the world, naked as it were.

After taking our leave of Doctor Morrison, Holmes and I walked the mile or so to the harbour where we were to catch the boat for Dieppe. The steamer was in her dock, the seamen preparing her for the voyage across the channel. Holmes grabbed my sleeve and whispered sharply into my ear. 'Watson, do you recognize the fellow at the barrier?'

I looked carefully and observed a small rat-faced man wearing a long coat and a bowler hat. 'Why, it is our old friend Lestrade. I wonder what he is doing down here?'

'I expect he is checking to see if you really have admitted me to the clinic. He is not altogether a fool, Doctor. His *copper's nose*

121

will have made him suspicious of us.'

Lestrade looked keenly about him, but if he recognized the elderly stooping nonconformist minister and the blue-suited gentleman in the gold-framed glasses as Sherlock Holmes and Doctor Watson, he gave no sign. Indeed he saluted us as we passed him by.

On board the ship we sat on a vacant bench and quietly discussed our plans and hopes.

'By the way, Holmes, or should I say, Vicar. Under what names shall we be travelling?'

'I am the Reverend Bull and you shall be Mr John Herbert, that is, if you have no objection to the usage of your middle name for our purposes?'

'No, indeed. It is far better to be known by a name that is familiar to one,' I said. 'Somehow it also makes me feel that it is less of a deception.'

Holmes laughed. 'Very good. Then the Reverend Bull and Mr John Herbert are on their way to France, for I perceive the boat is moving away from the jetty.'

FIVE

I awoke with a sudden start; for a moment I could not remember where I was. Then it came back to me. I was in a bunk on the night sleeper from Paris, bound for Lyons. I reached up and pulled the light switch cord above my head and the compartment was flooded with light. I looked at my watch, it was a little after six a.m. I supposed that it was very nearly time to be up and about, as the steward would be bringing my morning tea. Almost as if it had been preordained there was a light tap at the door.

'Enter,' I said.

A young man dressed in a white tunic stood there, tray in hand. He briskly wished me a good morning and informed me that the first seating for breakfast would be between seven and seven-thirty. If I so desired he would reserve me a place. Cognizant, not only of the old adage that to start the day properly one needs a substantial meal, but also knowing that there was the worrying (to my mind) prospect of missing out altogether, I readily agreed. As a consequence I was quickly at my toilet and had taken my seat well before the appointed hour.

I had hardly started on my egg when a familiar voice permeated the chatter of the other diners. 'Herbert. There you are, my dear fellow.'

'Reverend,' I cried. 'Please join me.'

Sherlock Holmes sat down on the seat opposite and addressed the hovering waiter. 'Just some coffee, if you please.'

He took out his pocket book and examined some notes he had made. 'I see that our train arrives at eight minutes past eight.' He took out his watch and looked at it. 'That is in twenty-eight minutes.' He replaced his watch and returned to his notes. 'The train from Lyons to Milan leaves just two minutes after our arrival. I sincerely trust that your digestive system will stand up to the inevitable jolt.'

I buttered a piece of toast and looked hopefully for the jam pot. 'At what o'clock do we arrive at Milan?'

Holmes turned the page of his notebook. 'At twenty minutes to two. And before you ask, Doctor, the Rome train leaves thirty minutes later.'

'Then it is just as well that I have provisioned for the day,' I cried triumphantly. 'For our schedule allows scant time for meals, or indeed anything else.'

Holmes laughed. 'Good old Watson.'

In Lyons we made the transfer to the Milan-bound train without difficulty or delay. The carriages were of an open design, with a wide walkway down the middle. Holmes had engaged two window seats and we sat smoking and watching the passing green fields with their trees in the process of bursting into life as the cycle of the year turned once more to growth and renewal. For a while, I sat in a brown study mulling over our mission and what we might find at the end of our journey. Sherlock Holmes leaned forward and tapped me on the knee with his pipe. 'You are distracted, Watson?'

'I was musing upon our errand, Holmes. Then it occurred to me that we are three parts across France, yet we have seen nothing of the sights of this wonderful country.'

Holmes frowned and nodded. 'Indeed. We have recently passed within twenty miles of my grandmother's birthplace. I would very much have liked to visit it and perhaps acquaint myself with some of her family.'

'My dear fellow,' I said quietly. 'I had no

idea. It is very unfortunate that our mission allows us no detour.'

'Ah yes,' he said. 'Our mission. You are right. The welfare of my brother Mycroft is of far greater importance than a foolish whim of mine.' He smiled. 'What whim of yours have we ignored, Doctor?'

'Well,' I said, thoughtfully. 'It would have been rather nice to see the great palace built by Louis XVI at Versailles, then look over Marie Antoinette's private village nearby.'

Holmes took out his vesta case, lit one and puffed on his pipe. Blowing smoke rings into the air he nodded. 'She was a sad creature, Watson. Quite unable to come to terms with the changing times in France, or with the tenuousness of her position.'

I said, 'Certainly in the case of Marie Antoinette, she suffered the ultimate price for failure. It cost her her head.'

As the train approached the Italian border, the terrain grew more mountainous. In the distance blue snowy pinnacles dodged in and out of high dark clouds. Holmes pointed to the north. 'There is Switzerland, Watson. I would have greatly desired to step once more upon the land which holds so many memories for both of us.'

For a short while there was silence. The year of 1891 was far into the past, yet I could still feel the very real sensation of hurt and anger I had experienced so many years before when realizing for the first time that my friend and companion had fallen to his death at the falls at Reichenbach, then later discovering that it had been an elaborate hoax. I saw Holmes watching me. There was a kindly expression in his eyes. 'My dear fellow,' he said gently. 'I see now that I have never fully understood the hurt and pain you have suffered. I see it now. I am so sorry.'

'The day when you disappeared was a truly lovely one.' I said wistfully. 'What was it Goethe wrote about Switzerland on days like that... "Her snow-capped peaks allowing Nature to whisper to us..."?'

Holmes chuckled. 'I seem to recall on that particular visit Nature, in the form of a waterfall, rather shouted at me.'

The border negotiated without difficulty, we now found ourselves in Italy. Holmes clearly approved of our present location. 'This is a place of great antiquity, Watson. Indeed, it is one of the few regions which can be said to have a longer and more distinguished history than our own.'

'But we have now surpassed Rome and

her might,' I said.

'It was only when our nation embraced capitalism that she emerged victorious in the world,' he replied.

'And with capitalism comes the insatiable advancement of materialism,' I objected.

Holmes reached forwards and poked me in the ribs with his pipe. 'Materialism is an essential part of our growth. Without it we become nothing. With it we may squeeze out of life our eventual salvation.'

I sighed. 'Holmes, I expect you are right. I cannot say, however, that I relish the prospect of such a world coming to pass.'

Holmes pulled a thoughtful face. 'With the fate of Europe on a knife-edge, my dear fellow, other factors may yet come into play. If war comes, as I fear it may, it will bring with it the end of many certainties. Yet it may also remove the uncertainties.'

'You believe that it will be war, Holmes?'

'I fear so, Watson. Did not Sir Arthur Richardson warn us that the Eagle thrones of Europe sit upon foundations which are about to crack?'

'What of the Empire?' I asked.

'What indeed. If it is to be war, then thousands of brave and loyal men from all four corners of the globe will come to the defence of their motherland. It will mean death and destruction for them, but it will also mean the preservation of the Empire.'

'Then the British crown is safe?'

'Without doubt. You see, Watson. His Majesty enjoys one particular and unique advantage over all other European monarchs. He rules, but he does not govern. Unlike Franz Joseph of Austria, Kaiser Wilhelm of Germany or Tsar Nicholas of Russia, the King is a constitutional monarch who rules with the consent of his people. He does not instigate legislation, he gives it his assent. His position is unique in Europe, King George is the stabilizing factor in our society and because of that he will not fall.'

'If you are to believe the newspapers, the other great powers are ruled by a dodderer, a lunatic and a fool, and rational decisions are beyond them. Then thank goodness for King George.'

Holmes nodded vigorously. 'Amen to that, Watson, and that is exactly why it so concerns me that the King and his ministers will be unable to influence his brother monarchs into sensible courses of action. But we must do what we can; and that is why we must rescue Mycroft. He may yet devise a solution. A key with which we can unlock the door to a lasting peace.'

Our journey continued without delay or incident. We had left Milan and were on the last leg to Rome. Some two hours had passed and my mind was turning to thoughts of dinner. The attendant had been round and had left us menus for the evening repast. Our discussion on the matter was suddenly interrupted, however, by the appearance of a tall dark-haired man in his early thirties. Clearly desirous of his remarks not being overheard, he bent his head towards Holmes and myself before speaking in little more than a whisper. 'Gentlemen. Please forgive this interruption,' he said, his voice betraying the merest hint of an accent. 'You're English?'

Holmes and I looked at each other.

'We are, sir,' said Holmes.

'Forgive me, sirs,' said the young man. 'I understand that I am interrupting your privacy, but there is a young Englishwoman, further down the train, who urgently requires your assistance.'

'I see,' said Holmes, gesturing to the visitor that he should sit down. 'May I enquire what precisely your interest in this matter might be?'

'Perhaps I had better explain myself. My name is Alfonso Cattini, *Capitano il Cara-*

binieri. I was passing by the private compartment when I observed a serious incident taking place in which a young woman was involved. Thinking it wise to intervene, I discovered that she was being accused of a serious offence, namely the stealing of a valuable necklace. When I learned that she was English, I thought perhaps her fellow countrymen might be willing to assist her.'

'Of course,' said Holmes.

The policeman signalled to one of the stewards who had been hovering in the middle distance. He spoke softly in Italian to the man who nodded his assent and made his exit to the rear of the train. Signor Cattini turned once again to Holmes and myself. 'Now, sir. The name of the English woman is Alice Ward. I do not know her age, but I judge her to be about twenty. She is in the employment of the Count and Countess of Vengloz. They are Bohemian, I believe. Miss Ward is employed as the personal maid of the Countess.

'I understand that Miss Ward was engaged in London, but she has worked for them in their Schloss near Lintz. Presently they are on their way to their summer retreat near Brindisi.

'Apparently, the Countess was dressing for

dinner and she asked Miss Ward to get her jewel box from the trunk. It was then that the Countess discovered her diamond necklace to be missing.

'At first it was supposed that for some reason of his own, the Count had removed the jewels and had simply forgotten to tell his wife. He had not touched the box, however, and it appeared that there was only one conclusion to be drawn. Someone had stolen the necklace.'

'Miss Ward was the chief suspect?' Holmes said quickly.

'Yes, sir. I am afraid so. If you exclude the Count and Countess. Miss Ward is the only person who has had access to the luggage.'

'Is the necklace of particular value, Captain?' I asked the policeman.

'The Count estimates the value to be somewhere in excess of five thousand of your pounds.'

'This is indeed a serious matter,' said Holmes thoughtfully. Gazing steadily at the policeman, he said. 'Tell me, as an officer of the law, how do you gauge Miss Ward and her employers?'

Captain Cattini sucked his teeth thoughtfully for a moment. 'Well, sir. I must confess to not liking the Count and Countess very much. They are arrogant and overbearing and I suspect that they treat Miss Ward with particular severity. As for the young lady herself, she is a tall, thin, even angular creature. It is without doubt that she is from a good family as she seems well educated and speaks excellent French. I think you English would best describe her with a French word, *Gauche*.'

Sherlock Holmes stood up. 'Very well, Signor Cattini. There is little more to say, therefore, let us look into this matter and see if we may uncover the truth.'

I followed Holmes and the captain through several busy coaches, then we entered the first-class compartments. Here the patrons enjoyed the luxury of separate accommodation. Suites rather than shared facilities were provided, privacy was the watchword.

The steward whom Signor Cattini had earlier dispatched, reappeared. He showed us into a brightly lit day cabin where three people sat waiting. One, a large, balding, corpulent man of late middle age, richly dressed and with an air of superiority about him; another, equally large, pasty-faced woman of a similar vintage to the man and equally well attired; the third, a thin pale young woman dressed in sensible clothes.

The man jumped to his feet and shouted angrily in English. 'Cattini. What is the meaning of this outrage? Why are we imprisoned in our own cabin? The culprit is known, why do you not arrest her and make her tell you where she has hidden the necklace?'

The policeman held up a hand. 'These are English gentlemen who have offered to assist me.'

Miss Ward glanced at Holmes. 'I have no need of spiritual help, sir,' she said drily.

Holmes smiled. 'I may be able to offer material assistance, madam.'

The Count said, 'What business is it of yours, sir?'

Holmes replied, 'Crime is the affair of all right-minded people, Count Vengloz.'

The Countess spoke to her husband in a language I did not recognize, but it was clear that she was asking him a question. Then she addressed Holmes in French. 'Sir, this matter really is no business of yours. My husband is mistaken. The necklace is not stolen. It is merely missing. This stupid girl has simply mislaid it.'

'Oh!' cried the young woman. 'That is not true. Just as the Count accused me, just now, the Countess accused me before this policeman.'

Signor Cattini appeared to be perplexed. Unable to speak any French he had found it impossible to follow the conversation. I swiftly translated for him.

'That is so, sir,' he said. 'The Countess called her a thief in English, although I understand that otherwise she speaks very little of the language.'

I sighed. This matter was serious enough without the unfortunate complication that none of the assembled shared a common language. All bar the Countess could speak English, she could speak French, whilst some of us could speak French, the Captain understood none.

Sherlock Holmes, however, was keen to swiftly investigate the matter. No language difficulties would stand in his way. He suggested a thorough search of the cabin inhabited by the Count and Countess and that of Miss Ward. The young woman was unequivocal in her reply to the suggestion. 'Certainly, I have nothing to hide.' Look where you will. When you return you will be empty handed.'

Taking Sherlock Holmes aside, I ventured the opinion that, as Miss Ward was quite happy to have her cabin searched, then she was quite probably innocent of any crime.

Holmes shook his head. 'Not so, my dear fellow. The young lady's invitation may merely indicate that the necklace is safely hidden in another place. She may simply be expressing bravado,' he smiled. 'However, Watson, the fair sex is your department and you may be right. Perhaps whilst I am undertaking my task, you may be inclined to discover something about Miss Ward.'

I invited Miss Ward into the first-class dining car. It was set for dinner, but as yet the dinners had not arrived so we sat at the table nearest to the exit, whilst Miss Ward told her something about herself.

'I am an orphan, sir. Save an elderly great aunt in Scotland, I have neither kith nor kin. My father died two years ago, my mother having pre-deceased him in 1900. I was at finishing school in Paris when he died. I also discovered that he was quite penniless, indeed the family home was heavily mortgaged to one of the private London banks. Unfortunately, the bank immediately foreclosed the mortgage and I was put out on the street.'

'My dear Miss Ward,' I said. 'What a terrible experience for one so recently bereaved.'

She laughed, but there was no humour in

her voice. 'It was an experience I would not care to repeat. It did, however, teach me a valuable lesson. The world does not owe one a living. It was more than a week before I could find a job. An agency eventually found me a position in one of the West End draper's shops at a salary of ten shillings a week. My living accommodation consisted of a room at a hostel for young ladies in Bayswater.'

'But how did you come to be in the employ of the Count and Countess?' I asked.

'It was by the purest of chance. One of the girls at the hostel worked at one of London's many small hotels. She always brought home with her a copy of a daily newspaper, provided as a courtesy for their patrons. I was idly turning the pages, when an advertisement for a lady's companion caught my eye.

'Reading further, it said that the ideal applicant should be of good education and speak French fluently, be single and under twenty-five years of age. Believing that I fulfilled all requirements, I begged from the dame the use of the hostel telephone and rang up the agency. I was given an appointment for the very next morning at ten a.m., at the Dorchester Hotel.

'Well, that night I borrowed some smart clothes from one of the girls and the next morning another put up my hair for me, so I would look sober and serious.

'At the Dorchester, I was met by a frosty-faced woman, Miss Porter, who had been appointed by the agency to weed out un-suitable applicants. After a quick perusal, she asked me for my details, which she wrote on a card with a number on the back and took me along to another room, where as I recall, six other young women, were waiting to be interviewed. I remember that each of them seemed to be far more attractive than me.'

I looked rather more closely at Miss Ward. She was not quite so plain and unattractive as I had at first thought. Undoubtedly she was both thin and gauche. I felt, however, that her thinness might be something to do with the Count and Countess, who whilst denying themselves nothing, probably kept her on the meanest of diets. She had nice teeth and a pleasant smile as a consequence. In all conscience, I could not see her as a thief.

'How did the interview proceed?' I said.

'I had some time to wait because I was the last applicant. When Miss Porter showed me into the room, the Count was sitting behind a large desk and the Countess sat huddled by the fire. It was a cold January day and she looked quite frozen. I answered the Count's questions, but he seemed to be less than enthusiastic. Then the Countess stood up and addressed him in their own language. After a few moments of animated discussion, the Countess smiled at me and said in French, "You are the best applicant, my dear. The Count does not find you particularly attractive, so you may begin your duties immediately.""

In spite of the seriousness of the present circumstances, I really had to smile. 'It appears that given the opportunity, the old boy has a penchant for a pretty girl. Did you feel insulted, Miss Ward?'

'Not sufficiently to turn down the position, sir,' she said wryly.

A few moments later Sherlock Holmes reappeared. His face bore more than a few traces of concern. Miss Ward jumped to her feet and looked urgently at him.

'Have you discovered anything that may prove my innocence, vicar?'

'No, Miss Ward. I have not. Neither have I uncovered anything that confirms your guilt.'

The young woman sat down once more, tears welling up in her eyes. 'Then the charge of theft still hangs over my head?'

Holmes nodded. 'I am sorry, Miss Ward,

but unless new evidence can be uncovered, the charge will hang over your head.' He smiled grimly. 'In the meantime, the Count has informed me that your employment has been terminated and you are free to return to London, when the train terminates in Rome.'

Miss Ward looked aghast at Sherlock Holmes. 'But what am I to do? I have done nothing wrong. Are you saying that if I am found to be innocent I am still dismissed?'

'It would appear so.'

I took the hand of the young woman and squeezed it gently. 'Holmes, surely there is something we can do? If indeed she is innocent and proved to be so, why should she be treated so shamefully?'

Holmes sighed. 'The Count and Countess are completely within their rights to terminate Miss Ward's employment. It is unfortunate that they have chosen to act in such a precipitous way, but that is their right. I am sorry, Miss Ward, in that I cannot help you.'

Miss Ward wiped her eyes. 'Reverend, I really do wish that I had stolen the necklace. It would have served them nicely for their harshness,' she said angrily.

'Who has taken the necklace?' I asked. 'Or is it merely mislaid? Have you no idea whatever?'

He shook his head. 'Without data, Herbert, I cannot say. All I am certain of, is the necklace is missing, there is no further evidence to hand.'

Captain Cattini looked in at the door. 'The steward tells me that they are about to serve dinner, gentlemen. Are you finished here?'

'Yes, Captain,' said Holmes, 'we are finished here. Miss Ward needs to collect her belongings from her old cabin. Will you escort her please?' He turned to me. 'In the meantime, Herbert, we have much to discuss. Let us find an unoccupied compartment for a council of war.'

I followed Holmes into a compartment and closed the door behind me. 'Now,' I said sharply. 'Are you of the opinion that Miss Ward is innocent?'

Holmes sat down and took out his cigarette case. 'Well, Watson, I am sorry to say that again there is insufficient data.'

'Then do you have any theories?' I persisted.

'I have theories in abundance,' he replied. 'I have considered five possible scenarios and, as yet, I cannot discount any of them.'

I sighed. Clearly getting to the truth was much harder than I had anticipated. 'But, what are we going to do with Miss Ward?' I demanded. 'Innocent or guilty, she is in need of assistance. At best she is now without any visible means of support. At worst she is facing some considerable time in an Italian gaol.'

There was a knock at the door and the head and shoulders of Captain Cattini appeared again.

'Sirs. There is fresh news. The necklace has been found.'

Holmes sat up in his seat. 'It has?'

'That is good news,' I said warmly.

Cattini frowned. 'I am not so sure, sir. Although the necklace has been recovered, several of the largest stones are missing.'

'Missing?' I cried.

Sherlock Holmes jumped up and grasped Cattini by the shoulder. 'Where was the necklace found, Captain?'

'If you will come with me, I shall show you.'

Holmes turned to me. His voice had a note of urgency in it. 'Herbert. Find Miss Ward and bring her with you to the Vengloz compartment. I shall meet you there presently.'

Somewhat mystified, I nodded my assent. As I made my way to the observation lounge where the captain had deposited Miss Ward, it occurred to me that there was something decidedly strange about the sudden discovery of the necklace. Surely Holmes would not have overlooked it. Had Miss Ward placed it on display when she collected her things, or had one of the Venglozes (or both of them) been responsible?

I looked in at the door to the observation lounge. There was Miss Ward; she was sitting, looking at the passing landscape, now covered with a veritable rash of vineyards, black stock just beginning to green up. I looked at the young woman sitting there with humped back, gangly and forlorn, viewing the scenery with sightless eyes, her fingers long and tapering, twisted into knots of worry.

She turned sharply at the sound of the opening door. Her worried face relaxed into a smile when she espied me. 'Is there any news?'

'Indeed,' I replied. 'The necklace has been found.'

She sighed loudly. 'Thank heavens. Then all is well.'

I shook my head. 'I am afraid not. Some of the diamonds are missing. The Reverend Bull wishes to see you in the first-class compartments to discuss the matter.'

Again her eyes filled with tears. I took out

my pocket-handkerchief and handed it to the distraught young woman. 'Come along, Miss Ward,' I said gently. 'You must compose yourself. Perhaps the Reverend Bull may yet provide evidence of your innocence.'

She looked at me with surprise in her eyes. 'You believe me to be innocent, sir?'

I took her hand and squeezed it gently. 'Yes, my dear. I believe I do.'

Miss Ward stood up and smiled. 'Then perhaps all is not lost. Let us join the Reverend Bull without delay.'

As we approached the first-class compartment, I could hear raised voices. Count Vengloz was arguing with Captain Cattini. When he espied Miss Ward and myself he became almost incandescent with rage. 'That girl. Why is she here?'

Holmes appeared from one of the cabins. 'Miss Ward is here to answer some questions.'

The young woman stiffened and looked at me with frightened eyes. 'What do you mean, vicar? Some questions?'

Holmes smiled at her. 'Please, wait here for a few moments. I have to speak briefly to Herbert. Then all will be revealed.'

He took my arm and pulled me into the next compartment. 'My dear fellow, something has happened which convinces me of

Miss Ward's innocence.'

'Holmes,' I cried. 'That is good news.'

'Indeed. Now, Watson, please escort Miss Ward to the first-class lounge. I shall bring the Count and Countess there myself. Then we will get to the bottom of this matter.'

The first-class lounge proved to be a particularly well-appointed carriage. Miss Ward and I sat down and waited. Sherlock Holmes arrived shortly after; clearly his powers of persuasion had proved to be sufficiently strong to convince the noble couple that they should attend. Holmes invited them to sit down opposite Miss Ward and myself. Captain Cattini brought up the rear and settled himself quietly by the exit.

There came a knock at the door and a steward appeared. He pushed before him a drinks trolley. In the middle of the cornucopia of spirits sat a large silver vessel full of crushed ice. On the undertray was a large plate of sandwiches which the steward placed on an adjacent table.

'As we seem to be missing our dinner, I thought it prudent to order some refreshment,' remarked Holmes. 'Oh, Count Vengloz,' he said turning to the nobleman. 'I had the steward borrow the ice bucket from your compartment. I hope you do not mind?'

'Ice?' I asked. 'Why should we need ice?'

'My dear fellow,' he cried. 'It is for our drinks. Have you not heard of this new fashion to have them cooled by ice in the glass? Why, it is all the rage in high society. Now,' he said pulling the trolley before him, 'who will have a drink with me?'

For myself, I was quite ready for a brandy and soda. Miss Ward shook her head, but the Count eagerly accepted Holmes's offer. Indeed he insisted on the mixing of the drinks. Whilst he had a whisky his wife selected a vermouth. Holmes had his usual brandy and soda. The Count dropped some ice into each of the drinks then handed them round. I took a sip. It was good.

'Now, sir,' said the nobleman to Holmes. 'What have you brought us here for?'

'I have asked for your attendance because I am about to unmask the felon who has stolen your wife's diamonds.'

'Good heavens. Then you know who is responsible?' I spluttered.

'Indeed.'

The Count snorted. 'There is no mystery here, Reverend. The thief is sitting just before you.'

'My dear Count Vengloz. How right you are,' said Holmes, his eyes blazing.

'Then put us out of our misery, for goodness' sake,' I cried.

'Presently,' said Holmes soothingly. 'Perhaps, however, I should explain how it was done.'

At this the Countess objected to the proceedings. Her English was so poor that she was experiencing difficulties in following the conversation. Despite the obvious antipathy between the two women, Miss Ward volunteered to translate the proceedings into French for her benefit.

'Now, Captain Cattini, when I was asked to investigate the theft of the necklace, you and I engaged ourselves in a thorough search, did we not?'

The policeman nodded and smiled. 'Oh yes. Never before have I seen such thoroughness. Why, the reverend gentleman poked and prodded into every conceivable corner.'

'And what did we find, sir?'

'We found precisely nothing.'

'Now. Some fifteen minutes later, you came across the necklace?'

'Yes. It was on top of the washstand in the bathroom. I had just escorted Miss Ward there to collect some of her belongings, and there it was. I cannot understand how we came to miss it.'

Holmes smiled thinly. 'No, Captain. But I can. That very washstand was one of the areas in which I made my search. The necklace was not there during my search. It had been placed there subsequently to incriminate another.'

'Miss Ward,' I said.

'Pah!' cried Countess Vengloz. 'The girl placed it there when she returned. She wanted to keep her job.'

'With six of the largest stones missing?' said Holmes evenly. 'I think not.'

The Count banged on the table with his fist. 'This is nonsense. Pure nonsense!'

The nobleman had it in his mind to say more, but one look from Sherlock Holmes quelled his desire. 'Now, Count. The thief is most certainly among us, but Miss Ward must be discounted. I am looking for another.' He held up his glass. 'But come, we have talked to excess and have not finished our drinks,' he smiled. 'Drink up and I shall tell you all.'

The spirit of Sherlock Holmes being far superior to ours, or indeed, the specific gravity of the contents of our glasses, we felt obliged to obey his request, therefore. I

148

reached for my glass, but as I raised it to my lips I discovered that the ice had melted away completely. I held out my drink to Holmes. 'My dear fellow, could I trouble you for some more ice?'

Holmes nodded and smiled.

'Of course, Herbert. Indeed I believe we must all need some fresh ice for our drinks. Except of course for the diamond thief... What do you say Count Vengloz?'

The Count gave a violent start.

'Count Vengloz!' I cried. 'He is the culprit.'

'Indeed,' Holmes answered quietly.

The Count's hand reached out for his glass, but Holmes was quicker. With a strike that an adder would have been proud of, he struck the glass from the table. It hit the floor and bounced, its contents scattering to all four corners of the lounge.

In an instant the Count was on the floor. On all fours he scrambled. Then he gave a cry of pain. Sherlock Holmes was standing on his hand. He smiled thinly at the discomfort of the nobleman, then reached down and picked up something. Throwing it upon the table, he remarked. 'There you are, Doctor. What do you make of that?'

'Why, it is only some ice,' I remarked, somewhat surprised by all the fuss. 'There is a whole bucket full of the stuff here.'

Holmes picked up the little crystal and held it out for my inspection. 'Are you quite sure it is ice?'

I took it from him and held it in my fingers for a moment. It was as hard as ice. It was wet from the drink. But it was not even cold.

'Well, it is certainly not ice. If not, then, what it is?'

'It is a diamond.'

'Good heavens.'

Miss Ward stood up and pointed an accusing finger at the Count. 'You wretch,' she cried angrily. 'Your treachery has almost cost me my freedom!' Then, without warning she picked up the ice bucket and threw it at the head of the bewildered nobleman.

Her aim was true and the ice bucket hit the Count fairly and squarely above the left ear and he fell to the floor as if pole-axed.

'Herbert,' said Holmes sharply. 'For goodness' sake, take Miss Ward away from here.'

Grabbing the young woman by the wrists, I half pushed, half pulled her across the ice-strewn lounge and into the relative calm of the connecting corridor. The door was opened for us by the steward. He had a broad smile on his face. He had observed Miss Ward's assault on Count Vengloz and was doubtless absorbing the event for later recapitulation to an assembly of his fellow workers.

Swiftly I propelled the angry young woman back to the observation lounge. Closing the door behind me with my foot and half expecting more fireworks, I tentatively released my grip on her. But she had calmed down; looking up at me, she smiled. 'I am sorry, sir. You need no longer fear my temper.'

'Good heavens, Miss Ward,' I remonstrated. 'You might easily have killed him.'

She raised an eyebrow and snorted. 'It would have almost served him right. He committed a crime and did his utmost to incriminate me. Also, do not forget, that although my name has been cleared, I am without employment, or indeed any visible means of support. If you ask me, a bang on the head with an ice bucket is a small price to pay for the wrong he has done to me.'

The hour had grown late when Holmes and I eventually sat down together for a pipe and a glass of something that cheers and inebriates. Dinner, although late, was a convivial affair. The matter of the stolen, or rather borrowed, diamond necklace had been fully explained by Sherlock Holmes to a rapt audience, comprising of Miss Ward, Captain Cattini and myself.

The captain took out his cigarettes and lit one. He puffed away appreciatively. 'Now, sir,' he said. 'We are all waiting for a full explanation. Just how did you unmask the Count?'

Holmes laid his pipe on the table before him and sat back in his seat. He looked keenly at the policeman. 'The Count and Countess Vengloz are a noble couple; his family has connections to Bohemian and south German kingdoms. Yet despite this relationship, the family has little money. They have done their best to keep up appearances, but it has been a losing battle. They travel first class as befits their status, but they scrimp and scrape in other areas. Miss Ward, I believe, has a nominal salary, but is yet to see a penny of it. The staff on this train have waited on the couple hand and foot, so to speak, but have yet to feel the weight of a gratuity slipped into their hand.

'It may interest you to know that the Countess has admitted to me that the jewels she wears with such ostentation, are almost without exception, paste. Indeed, the diamond necklace at the centre of this affair is the one truly valuable item in the Countess's jewel box.

'Presently the creditors have been pressing the Count for payment and it seemed possible that legal proceedings were in the offing. Then quite recently, the Count's secretary added to the family problems by insisting that valuables owned by them should be properly insured, particularly as many of them would be travelling with the Count and Countess on their annual summer trek to Brindisi.

'Initially the Count stood out against further expenditure, but the secretary persisted. What would happen if the jewels were stolen? Who would replace them? Judging by the state of his bank balance, not the Count. Then it occurred to the Count that there could be a way out of his financial difficulties. The necklace was worth perhaps five thousand pounds. It had been given to his wife by a minor Bohemian noble and was an original Fabergé. So perhaps if the necklace were stolen on route to Brindisi the insurance money would provide an avenue back to solvency.

'Accordingly, it was today that the Count took the necklace from his wife's jewel box. It was done in the full knowledge that it would be Miss Ward, his wife's personal maid, who would be the prime suspect for the crime. He prised out the seven most valuable diamonds and pocketed them. The necklace, he intended to throw out of the window at the first convenient opportunity.

'Choosing his moment carefully the Count staged a scene, which he knew would attract outside interest. It was then when the Count suffered his first stroke of ill-fortune, when you, Captain, called upon Wat – upon Herbert, and myself.'

'The Count abandoned the idea of simply throwing away the remains of the necklace. He waited until I had completed my search, then he slipped into the dressing room and placed the remains of the necklace upon the washstand. He hoped that its sudden appearance would be put down either to carelessness on the part of the searchers or more probably at the door of Miss Ward who had recently returned to collect her belongings.

'This was the Count's second stroke of ill-fortune. It was I who had searched the dressing room. Such an elementary oversight on my part was simply not possible. The Count had hoped that I would jump to the conclusion that Miss Ward was the culprit. Well, as I explained earlier, Herbert, this was one of five scenarios in my mind.

'When I returned to the Vengloz compartment, the Count put on a fine show of annoyance, and when Miss Ward reappeared at my invitation, he became quite overwrought. Whilst I was attempting to calm him down, I discovered the singular fact, that whilst his left hand was quite normal in temperature, his right was extremely cold, indeed it was icy cold.

'I considered this particularly odd. Why should this be? It was then, when I first espied the ice bucket on the table. I concluded that for some reason the Count had just plunged his hand into the crushed ice. But why? Then it was, as the poet says, *"the mists of obfuscation"* cleared and the bright sunlight of truth shone through.'

Holmes laughed and tapped his pipe on the ashtray. He looked questioningly at his audience and said, 'He had secreted something in the ice.'

'The diamonds!' I cried.

'Herbert. You excel yourself. The diamonds it is. When they are surrounded by ice they are hard to distinguish, indeed invisible to the casual observer.'

I laughed. 'And that is why you staged that ridiculous charade with the drinks trolley.'

'Indeed. It was a subterfuge designed to force the Count's hand. If, as I expected, he had plunged a handful of diamonds into the ice, he would be needful of removing them as quickly as possible.'

'So that is why the Count was so very keen to assist you with the drinks,' said the captain.

'Exactly. He had to ensure that the diamonds ended up in his own glass.' Holmes refilled his pipe. 'Quite realizing the Count's dilemma, I engaged the assembly in a prolonged conversation. The ice in everyone else's drink quickly melted, but the Count's drink stayed completely unchanged. Our case was proven.'

Captain Cattini looked troubled. 'But why did Count Vengloz feel it to be necessary to place the necklace on the washstand? He surely must have realized that he was taking a risk?'

'Oh indeed,' said Holmes. 'He hoped that we would regard it as an oversight.'

It was a little after one a.m. when at last I stepped down onto the platform in Rome. The train was not very full, but Holmes and myself decided to wait a little and avoid what rush there might be. As I stood there in the high vaulted building, waiting for the baggage to be deposited, I noticed Count and Countess Vengloz descending from their first-class compartment. The Count appeared to be struggling with several heavy-looking bags. A number of stewards and other personnel were standing about chatting idly, but none appeared to take any particular interest in the Count's predicament. Apparently the general tightfistedness of the Venglozes and their disdainful attitude to the stewards had come home to roost with something of a vengeance.

Sherlock Holmes appeared. Behind him, like some Arabic *caravansarai*, trailed a string of porters, huffing and puffing with the collective baggage of our little party.

Miss Ward and Captain Cattini stepped down from the carriage, the captain helping her down the last high step. Suddenly, the Countess detached herself from the growing pile of baggage. She waved and began to trot towards us.

'Good heavens,' I said, as the plump noblewoman made her approach. 'What does she want?'

It was Miss Ward whom apparently was the object of the lady's desire.

'My dear,' she said, in a quavering voice.

'You have little to thank us for, I am sure, but please hear me out. The Count and I have treated you most shamefully, yet you have refused to press charges. You have shown a nobility of spirit that neither of us, with all our high connections, could ever hope to achieve.' There were tears in her eyes as she held out a small package. 'Please take this. It is given in the hope that it may prove to be some small recompense for the suffering you have undergone.'

Without another word, the Countess turned on her heel and returned to the growing chaos which surrounded her husband.

'Well,' said Miss Ward. 'What do you make of that? And what do you suppose is in the box?'

I raised my eyebrows and shook my head. 'I imagine that the only way in which you will discover that is by opening the box,' I said.

Miss Ward lifted the lid and gave a cry of surprise and astonishment. 'Look!' she cried.

She held out the box. Inside was a crumpled piece of pink tissue; nestling in the tissue was a small glittering diamond.

'Remarkable,' said Holmes. 'Quite remarkable.'

Miss Ward departed, and Holmes and I were looking round for a carriage, when suddenly Captain Cattini appeared, as if from nowhere.

'Captain?' I asked anxiously. 'Is anything wrong?'

'Not wrong, Mr – ah, Herbert,' he told me, with a sardonic glint in his eye. 'But there is, I think, a little puzzle. If you would be so kind?' And he took us into a dark and poky little office, and closed the door.

'Now, gentlemen, grateful as I am for your help with this sordid affair, one question remains to be answered. Just who are you? For I tell you frankly, I never met a priest or a vicar with such strange skills as the Reverend Mr Bull.'

Holmes and I exchanged a glance. Then Holmes said, 'In confidence, then, I am Sherlock Holmes, and this is Doctor John Watson. We are in disguise, and upon a secret mission of the greatest delicacy. You understand?'

'Sherlock Holmes! And Doctor Watson!' Cattini stared at us for a long moment, then nodded his head. 'Ah, yes. Now I understand. I understand perfectly.'

SIX

It was a little after one a.m. when at last we reached the outskirts of Rome. The journey from Milan had seemed quite intractable. Sherlock Holmes had telegraphed His Majesty's Ambassador to Italy, in his own name. In his view, the time for secrecy and subterfuge had passed. The communication contained Holmes's grave doubts about the report of his brother's untimely death and a request that the ambassador should be ready to meet and assist us in our quest to rescue Mycroft from the clutches of the scoundrels running the Bixio Clinic.

In spite of the lateness of the hour, the city was ablaze with light and colour. It was almost as if the citizens were organizing a special show for their visitors. Our driver, however, quickly dispersed any such illusions. 'Ah, *Signor*. The Romans, they parade each night. They show off their finery like peacocks.'

'Hm...' I mused. 'How on earth do they manage to be up next morning to carry on with their commerce?'

The driver laughed. 'They manage, *Signor*. They manage.'

Before long we were rattling our way through the open gates of the ambassador's residence. Here too the lamps were lit. Clearly we were expected. As Holmes and I jumped down from the carriage, the front door opened and we were bathed in a pool of light; standing in the doorway was a tall, well-built figure of a man, his frame thrown into sharp relief by the light behind him. He stepped forward and stood in the diffused light of the residential steps. It was then, for the first time, I clearly saw his face.

'Good Lord! It's Jimmy!'

It was indeed General James Wilton. 'Hello John ... Mr Holmes, welcome to the eternal city.'

Until that moment, I had always taken the view that when someone who had just had a great surprise, reported that they could have been knocked down with a feather, it had to be pure hyperbole. Now, however, I knew it to be the literal truth. Indeed, if anything, it was a complete understatement.

'But... What are you doing in Rome?' I stuttered.

'Awaiting your arrival, John.'

Sherlock Holmes said nothing. He merely looked grim. Wilton showed us into a large well-appointed room which clearly was his personal study. All around us were certificates and mementoes, which spoke of a career in the service of our country. A side table, well provided with food and drink, stood by the fire. General Wilton selected a bottle and held it up for our inspection. 'You will enjoy this, gentlemen. It is a Chianti.'

'You were expecting us,' I said. 'But where is the ambassador?'

My old army colleague smiled. 'It is I, John. General James Wilton, His Majesty's Ambassador to Italy.'

As usual, Sherlock Holmes was in no mood for trivial conversation. 'How long have you been aware of our mission, General?'

'Do not concern yourself, Mr Holmes. I am the only person in Rome, or in London for that matter, who is in possession of the facts. There is no doubt the whole of London believes you to be either mad or in the grip of some malady.'

The general poured three glasses of wine. 'Oh, Mr Holmes. Your request for that merchant ship to be impounded and searched when it arrives in Naples? You will be pleased to know that the authorities have agreed to co-operate. If your Mr Andrews is on board, the Carabinieri will find him.' He handed the wine round and looked questioningly at Holmes. 'What I do not understand, Mr Holmes, is the need for such subterfuge. I must say, back in London my soldier's instinct for the truth troubled me. I suspected some kind of ruse, but for the life of me, I couldn't see what you were up to. Now I know. You are in Italy because you suspect some foul deeds up at the Bixio Clinic. But I'm frankly at a loss to understand much more.'

Sherlock Holmes looked sharply at General Wilton. 'It is quite evident to me, sir, that there is a great deal about this matter you do not understand, although I believe the malady stretches all the way back to London. So let me clearly state my objective. Certain evidence in my possession convinces me, that my brother is not dead... At least, not yet. I believe for the present he is being kept under guard at the clinic. Now, General, the matter of keeping Mycroft alive is paramount. I needed to maintain the status quo and had to act in any way I could to delay the meeting of the international conference. If it does not meet, Mycroft is safe. When it is finally convened he becomes surplus to requirements and he will surely be killed.

'I was to replace my brother. Now I am *hors de combat*, the government has failed to find a suitable replacement, so there is an inevitable hiatus and that allows me time to investigate the Bixio Clinic and free my brother from the clutches of his captors. Is everything now clear to you, sir?'

'Will you assist us in this undertaking, Jimmy?' I asked.

The general raised his hands in a gesture of defeat. 'I am not at all sure there is much I can do to intervene into what, in effect, are the private affairs of an Italian establishment. I may be His Majesty's Ambassador, but my powers in this direction are extremely limited. All I can do is request that the clinic prepare the supposed body of your brother for repatriation to his mother country and if, as you say, Mr Holmes, they are playing some nefarious game, they may delay for as long as possible.'

Holmes banged his glass down onto the table and fixed the general with a cold stare. 'It is quite clear, sir, permission for you or indeed anyone to visit the clinic will not be given until Mycroft is dead, which unless we act quickly, he most certainly will be very soon. It is inevitable that His Majesty's government will shortly announce a substitute to represent Great Britain at the conference. As soon as the disclosure is made, Mycroft's life is forfeit.'

Wilton looked grimly at Holmes. 'It is no secret that a replacement has been sought, but I do not know what I can do to assist you, Mr Holmes,' he said, waving his hands in a gesture akin to a manacled man. 'My hands in this matter are quite securely tied.'

'Pah!' cried Holmes. 'On many an occasion I have worked outside the law and this enterprise will be no exception,' he said as he poked the general in the waistcoat with a long bony forefinger. 'If you really desire to assist us, sir, let me suggest that you make available a carriage and a member of your staff you can trust in a tight corner, who can translate for us where necessary.'

Wilton smiled and rubbed his chin reflectively. 'You intend to go through with your plan?'

'I do.'

'By Jove, Holmes. There are times when I wish I was still a simple soldier. This is undoubtedly an adventure I once would have undertaken with relish.'

I smiled back at my old army colleague.

This was the fellow I remembered. The man of decision and action, rather than the diplomat he had become. 'Jimmy, if you know a fellow who can be relied on, we would be most grateful.'

The general picked up a small brass bell from an occasional table and shook it. Almost immediately the door opened and a servant appeared. 'Send Milan to me.'

The servant bowed and departed.

'The fellow I have sent for is regarded by the rest of the staff here as something of an odd fish. He's a Slav, I believe, but he speaks both English and Italian beautifully.'

A few moments later there came a firm knock at the door followed by the entrance of a tall swarthy man with black curly hair. His black intelligent eyes quickly swept the room.

'Ah, Milan. These gentlemen require your assistance. Do you understand?'

'*Si, Signor Generale*. I understand,' he said smiling at us.

'It is a secret matter.'

He laughed. 'When people send for Milan, it usually is.'

Sherlock Holmes took our new companion by the arm and propelled him over to the fire. For a few moments they conversed in low tones. Then Milan laughed again and slapped Holmes on the back. 'Mr Holmes. As you say in England, I am your man. If you tell Milan what to do, he will do it for you.'

And so it was, little more than half an hour later, that Holmes, Milan and myself were rattling through the dark and shadowy streets of Rome in a carriage en route to the Bixio Clinic, some four miles to the south of the city.

Sherlock Holmes reached into his pocket and took out a box of vestas. He struck one and looked at his watch. It was a little after four a.m. He blew out the match and once more we were plunged into darkness. Only the stars above now lit our way.

Milan pulled up the horses and pointed to a light that was perhaps half a mile in the distance. 'There, the Bixio Clinic. I think it best that we walk from here.'

'Indeed,' agreed Holmes. 'We certainly do not wish to warn our enemies of our approach.' He climbed down from the carriage. 'Come, Watson. Our adventure begins.'

Our path to the clinic proved to be very uneven, and on at least two occasions I stumbled and almost fell.

'This is a fine undertaking,' I remarked peevishly. 'Goodness knows this is adventure enough for a young man, but at fifty-seven I am becoming distinctly weary of adventures.'

Holmes grunted. 'When Mycroft is free and we are all safely back in England, I promise you, Watson, there will be no more adventures.'

A high whitewashed wall, topped with metal spikes loomed up out of the darkness. It was clearly the perimeter wall of the clinic. A little way along the wall was the source of the light. A small lamp was hanging over double wrought iron gates and the light it shed was sufficient for me to see the sign *'Bixio Clinic'* and the heavy chain and padlock wrapped securely around the gates.

'Well now,' I said. 'Which do we climb over, the wall or the gates?'

Holmes chuckled softly. 'Neither, my boy. Not whilst I still possess my tool kit.'

From an inside pocket he produced a small leather pouch. It was an item I had seen him employ many times during our long association. He selected a brass tool of particular fineness and proceeded to pick the lock. Moments later there came a sharp click and the padlock came apart.

For Milan, this was a new and entertaining experience. 'Ha ha! Mr Holmes, you would make an excellent housebreaker.'

Gently, Holmes swung open one of the gates. Fortunately for us the clinic believed in the good maintenance of their property for the gate swung on silent hinges.

'Now,' said Holmes crisply. 'If we can only find an open window.'

Milan was very soon able to prove his credentials as a housebreaker as well. He quickly discovered a window with a faulty catch. Signalling for Holmes and myself to follow him, he took from his belt a large knife with a strong tapering blade. Jumping up onto the sill, he quickly forced the catch. Moments later we found ourselves inside the Bixio Clinic.

The room in which we found ourselves was small and quite empty. The egress was easy to find because a faint glow permeated from the other side of the door.

Cautiously, Holmes turned the handle and pulled open the door. He peered out. 'We are in luck, there is no one about.'

Milan and I followed Holmes into a corridor. A little night-light was glowing on a small table. It gave off sufficient illumination for me to observe my surroundings. Beneath my feet lay a deep blue carpet. The walls were lined with expensive-looking paintings. It was at this juncture that something occurred to me. I gently nudged Holmes. 'There is something not quite right here,' I whispered.

'Indeed?'

'Have you noticed the lack of antiseptic smell one normally associates with clinics and hospitals?'

Holmes pulled a thoughtful face. 'Yes, you are quite right, Watson, and that only confirms our suspicions.'

Suddenly, from somewhere in the distance, there came the sound of a door opening and closing. The next moment a large swarthy man appeared from around the corner. He was wearing a khaki uniform. Here without doubt was an Italian militiaman.

His hand moved for the pistol on his belt. But if the militiaman was quickly into action, Milan was quicker. He threw himself at the man's legs bowling him over. Down in a heap they fell. After a brief struggle Milan rose to his feet brandishing the stricken militiaman's pistol and wearing a huge grin.

'My dear fellow,' I muttered.

The man was quickly deposited in the empty room we had recently vacated. Bound by his own belt and gagged by his own bandanna, he would no longer represent a danger to our liberty. For his uniform, we found an excellent use. It was quite remarkable how suited to it Milan seemed.

Holmes had seen immediately how to use this unforeseen stroke of luck to our best advantage. Milan would lead Holmes and myself, pistol in hand. Should we be approached by a member of staff or a militiaman, we would be Milan's prisoners captured by him whilst attempting to break into the clinic.

Milan led us through the same door, through which our victim had recently come. We found ourselves in another dimly lit corridor. This led into a large atrium with a flight of red carpeted marble stairs at one end and a set of heavy doors, which was clearly the main entrance, at the other. Above us was a balustraded balcony, which ran around the other sides from the stairhead. As before, the area was lit by night lights which enabled me to see that the walls were hung with more beautiful paintings and they were lined by exquisite marble figures and *objet d'art*.

I looked wryly at Holmes. 'Well, whatever their business is, it certainly seems to pay them well.'

Milan, who had been carefully inspecting the doors leading from the main hall, whispered urgently. 'Mr Holmes. Here is the place you need.'

'Excellent,' said Holmes. 'The director's office.'

Fortunately the door was unlocked and we were able to gain a quick and easy access. Milan swiftly pulled the curtains. Holmes once more took out his vesta case and struck one. He lit the lamp on the desk. 'Now, we have the light we need to progress.'

On the desk was a file that contained a list of names. Holmes quickly inspected it. 'This is no use, Watson. We need to find the names of those who are incarcerated here. But I am hampered by my poor Italian.'

Milan picked up the discarded document and quickly read it. 'This is a staff rota, Mr Holmes.' He pointed to a large wooden cabinet with several deep drawers. 'That must be where the information we require is kept.'

'Watson,' said Holmes crisply. 'Will you please keep watch by the door, someone may come along at any moment.'

'Yes, of course, Holmes.'

Holmes signalled for Milan to join him by the cabinet. Again he took out the leather pouch and selected a suitable tool. Moments later the lock operated with a sharp click. At Holmes's command, Milan rifled through the files. Eventually he discovered the document he was seeking.

Milan looked at Holmes with a disappointed face. 'I am sorry, but I cannot find any reference to your brother, Mr Holmes. Are you sure he is here?'

'He is here,' said Holmes. 'Mycroft must be incarcerated under an alias.' He took the document from Milan. 'Show me the list of names, if you please.'

'Certainly. There are three people registered here. One, Signor Bucci. Two, Signora Taracelli. Three, Signor Nimo.'

Holmes thumped his right fist into the palm of his left hand. 'Of course... It is Signor Nimo... – Mr No-one. Which room is he in, Milan?'

Milan looked once more at the file. 'He is in room twenty-six.'

'There is a chart of the rooms here, Holmes,' I said.

Sherlock Holmes took up the lamp and peered closely at the chart. 'Good old Watson. Mycroft is to be found upstairs and at the back of the clinic.'

Milan took the lamp from Holmes and

replaced it on the desk. He quickly extinguished it and we once more found ourselves in the half light. I opened the door and cautiously peered out. Milan quickly ran past me and to the bottom of the marble stairs, then the top; he quickly surveyed the area. Then he signalled that all was well and we should follow him.

A short way along the corridor, we came to a door behind which we heard a considerable amount of talking and laughing. Milan listened closely for a few moments. 'They seem to be playing cards,' he said.

Then at last we stood before the door of room twenty-six. Sherlock Holmes gestured for us to be silent. Cautiously he turned the handle. The door was unlocked. Gently, Holmes pushed the door open and peered inside. To my surprise, he gave a little cry of joy and threw the door open wide.

There, inside the room, was a desk, a chair and a glass-panelled booth. In the booth two figures lay. One, a large portly man, was on the bed; the other, a militiaman, was lying on the floor. The large man sat up and keenly observed us with grey piercing eyes. 'Hello, Sherlock, my dear,' he said. 'So you have come for me at last?'

Holmes strode across to the bedside of his

brother. 'My dear fellow.'

A look of tenderness was exchanged between the brothers. Then, the moment was past. Mycroft Holmes gestured towards Milan and myself. 'You have brought reinforcements, Sherlock?'

'Indeed ... Watson you know ... and this stout fellow is...'

'...Milan Spasich,' interrupted Mycroft. 'Milan is known to all diplomats who visit Italy. He is quite indispensable to us.'

Mycroft Holmes slipped off the bed and walked in a rather stiff and uncomfortable manner towards the stricken militiaman.

'What has happened to you, sir?' I asked.

'I'm afraid my captors have used me rather roughly, Watson. A case of not wisely but too well.'

An angry glint came into the eye of Sherlock Holmes. 'Perhaps they may yet have the opportunity to take some of their own medicine,' he said darkly.

'What has become of your captor, sir?' I asked the elder Holmes.

Mycroft Holmes chuckled. 'This poor fellow is a victim of his own sleeping draughts.' He bent down and gripped the sleeve of the stricken man. The man's arm moved limply up and down, then, as Mycroft released his grip, it fell to the floor with a thudding noise.

'For several nights I have complained of insomnia, so for the last three evenings I have been given something to make me sleep. Of course I did not take the soporific, but concealed it for later usage.

'Tonight, I offered my poor simple friend, who is sleeping so soundly there, a glass of vino tinto, which I had laced liberally with sleeping draughts. He is a simple soul and tricking him was as easy as shooting fish in a barrel.'

'Well now, brother,' said Holmes briskly. 'Let us hope that the remainder of our venture will prove to be as simple as your soldier.'

Once more we entered the corridor. As before, Milan took the lead, Holmes and I assisted Mycroft, who was still a little unsteady on his feet.

Suddenly the door to the militiamen's room swung open and several men in uniform spilled out into the corridor. They were clearly quite intoxicated, but they were still able to discern intruders. The one nearest to Milan shouted to his companions. *'Avanti,'* he cried. *'Dove la garda?'* He raised his gun and pointed it at us. 'Stop.'

Unfortunately for the militiaman, Milan

did not stop. He threw himself at the man and brought him crashing to the floor. The violence of Milan's assault sent the Slav and the Italian tumbling into the other militiamen.

Holmes made as if to assist him, but Milan shouted at him to desist. 'No, Mr Holmes. Go ... go before the whole clinic is in uproar. I will join you shortly!'

Taking Milan at his word, Holmes and I took an arm each and propelled Mycroft towards the stairs. Then from behind us came a bright flash quickly followed by a loud report and a considerable amount of dust and debris.

Down the stairs we ran, half-dragging Mycroft in our wake. 'The main entrance,' Holmes cried. 'We no longer need concern ourselves with subterfuge.'

The inner doors were unlocked and Holmes threw them open, the main door, however, was securely fastened.

'Your revolver, Watson.'

I fired several rounds into the lock. The wood splintered and fragments flew in several directions. By now the air was full of dust, smoke and the stench of cordite and from somewhere in the distance I could hear the sound of running feet.

Sherlock Holmes heaved at the broken door and it opened slightly. Squeezing himself into the gap, he forced the door half open, seized Mycroft and pulled him through the gap. Quickly I followed him. Then for a moment, I turned and looked back.

'Watson!' cried Holmes. 'For goodness' sake, man, hurry!'

'Coming, Holmes. Coming. I am looking out for Milan.'

Holmes was instantly by my side. 'We cannot delay. If Milan survived the blast, he must doubtless be injured. If we delay, his immolation will have been in vain.'

From somewhere in the smoky chaos, there came the sound of gunfire. A bullet smacked into the woodwork just above my head. The situation had become decidedly dangerous and I thrust myself through the opening once more and back out into the cool night air.

By now the moon was up and we could see each other quite clearly.

Holmes held up a large stave he had found goodness knows where. 'Here, Watson. Jam this into the frame. It will impede our enemies for a time.'

I did as I was instructed and quickly followed Holmes and Mycroft into the compound. All along the front of the clinic, I could see lights coming on. As I looked up, smoke began to drift from the roof. Then an upstairs window exploded and a red tongue of flame burst out into the night. Milan had clearly started a fierce conflagration.

Again, I could hear the sound of running feet. Fortunately, Mycroft seemed to have finally found his sea legs and he was able to keep up with Holmes and myself. Through the main gateway we ran, then Holmes suddenly stopped.

'Holmes!' I cried.

'Watson, escort Mycroft to the carriage and wait there for me. I shall be only a moment. But for goodness' sake, keep to the shadows.'

Somewhat confused, I obeyed him, and a few moments later we were in sight of the vehicle. Then Mycroft tugged at my sleeve and cried out. 'Look, Watson. There is someone in the seat.'

'They have located us,' I said grimly. 'That is unfortunate.' Once more I drew my revolver. 'But, it will be more unfortunate for him. Follow me, Mr Holmes, we shall soon remove the fellow.'

Suddenly Sherlock Holmes was at my side. 'Where have you been?' I demanded.

'Merely obstructing our pursuers a trifle,' he said airily.

'What on earth do you mean?'

'Let us say that a lock can both be picked and unpicked,' he smiled. 'I expect our friends are this very moment seeking the key to the padlock on the main gate.' From behind us there came a long burst of gunfire.

'Ah, I believe they seem to be approaching the lock in the same manner as yourself.'

I pointed to the man sitting on the seat in our carriage. Holmes grimaced. 'It would seem, Watson, that we have one more obstacle to overcome before making our bid for freedom.'

Then the man stood up and looked around and for the first time I clearly saw his face.

'Good lord, it is Milan ... Milan!'

Hearing my voice, Milan shouted out, 'Quickly, Doctor Watson, over here! We have very little time.'

Milan jumped back into his seat and goaded the horses into life. In a trice Holmes, Mycroft and myself joined him in the carriage.

It was not a moment too soon. There came a further burst of gunfire. On this occasion

I could see flashes of light from the muzzles. Our pursuers were no more than thirty feet from our vehicle. Bullets sang past my head as we raced away from the Bixio Clinic. Then, moments later, we had turned onto the road for Rome. The rescue of Mycroft Holmes was complete and we had escaped virtually unscathed.

SEVEN

I sat up in bed and looked at my watch. It was past nine o'clock, a disgraceful hour to be abed. Considering the lateness of the hour when I had eventually tumbled into the arms of Morpheus, however, I felt disinclined to reproach myself.

There came a light knock at the door. It was one of the embassy servants. He placed a tray on the side table and pulled the heavy curtains. *'Bonjourno, Signor Doctor. Com'e sta?'*

Recalling the smattering of Italian I had managed to acquire, I replied. *'Bene, grazi!'*

I inspected the tray. So this represented the standard Italian fare. No eggs, kidneys, bacon, sausages or tomatoes. No porridge and certainly no tea! It occurred to me that it was little wonder the continental personality was quite so excitable. For who could start the day on such unprepossessing fare as coffee and rolls and continue to remain both calm and composed?

A little later, after I had completed my ablutions, I came down into the guest morning room. Of my companions there was no sign. So for a short while I perused a week-old copy of *The Times* newspaper.

I had all but done, when I casually referred to the newspaper leader article. There, in large type, I observed a most singular and troublesome headline that caused me to study the opinion and conclusions drawn by the editor in an article I now wholly reproduce.

THE GREAT HOLMES MYSTERY

There is something devilish afoot these days, and it is not confined to the pages of that most excellent periodical, *The Strand Magazine*; It is happening at this precise moment in the very real world about us.

Something rather odd and quite strange seems to have befallen the brothers Holmes. The genius of these remarkable siblings is well known and much envied in some quarters. It has even been said that the hand of God has touched Sherlock and Mycroft. Whilst that is surely hyperbole, it is un-deniable that their activities have engendered an enormous effect on this great nation. Sherlock for his celebrated ability to clear our streets of master criminals; and Mycroft, whom for many years has been something in the government, and on several celebrated occasions has acted to prevent conflict between the great powers. But now, after a lifetime of public service, these two giant intellects seem to have simply dropped out of sight. Sherlock, we understand, has recently succumbed to a bout of melancholia and is supposed to be presently residing at a clinic for mental invalids. His elder brother, how-ever, has simply vanished without trace.

The question on the lips of all newspaper-men, hack and essayist alike, is, 'Sherlock and Mycroft, what are you really working on?' We know the European situation is rather uncertain and events may propel us into an international war. We ask, therefore, 'Where are Sherlock and Mycroft?' Are they intervening to draw our continent back from the brink? Or have the pressures of life finally caused them to desert this great

183

nation in her hour of need?

We believe our people have a right to know.

Somewhat surprised and stunned by the direction and closeness of the editor's questions, I folded the newspaper and threw it down upon the table. The door opened. It was Sherlock Holmes. He looked grim. 'Watson, old fellow. It would seem our success rate has been rather less than adequate. The *Pride of Thanet* docked last night in Naples, but of our Hunter Andrews there was no sign. Somehow his captors have conspired to elude our net.'

I picked up the newspaper again and pointed out to Holmes the article I had just read.

'Hm... It would seem that the fates have decided to obstruct our contrivances,' he muttered. 'It is fortunate, however, that the rescue of Mycroft means at least Britain is now able to go to the international conference and put into place those plans to which this newspaper alludes,' he smiled briefly. 'It also means we will now be able to go about our own affairs unfettered and undisguised.'

I looked doubtfully at Holmes. 'Does this mean I will at long last, be able to grow back my moustache?'

'Yes, Watson,' he said, 'I believe it does.'

There was a light tap at the door and an official of His Majesty's government stood there. 'Excuse me, gentlemen. The ambassador wishes to speak with you. If you will please follow me?'

We were shown into a small but lavishly appointed office. Despite the warmth of the day, a fire crackled merrily in the grate. Then a door, which had been concealed in the bookcase, opened and General Wilton and Mycroft Holmes stepped into the room.

'Gentlemen,' said the general. 'I hope you slept well?'

'Good morning, Doctor Watson, Sherlock,' said Mycroft. 'I'm afraid your little escapade last night has resulted in some unpleasant consequences.'

The general sat down at his desk and opened a file, which had been awaiting his attention. 'Mr Holmes is considerably understating the case. The Italian government is furious with you. Not only did you burgle a private clinic, you attacked and injured several of its personnel; and into the bargain you almost managed to burn it to the ground.' He sighed as he turned the pages. 'Your activities have made you *per-*

sonas non gratas in Italy. Fortunately I have managed to convince the Minister of the Interior that yours was a freelance escapade and His Majesty's government neither supports, nor condones, your activities.' The general held up a sheet of foolscap paper with a coat of arms emblazoned upon it. 'This is your notice of deportation and with it comes the severest motion of censure, I, as Britain's ambassador, can issue. You have one week to leave the country.'

General Wilton sat back in his chair and looked at Holmes and myself with keen eyes. 'Do you realize?' he said, 'that between yourselves and that madman Milan Spasich, you damn near destroyed that clinic. You may have proved your point, Mr Holmes, but your adventure has all but wrecked international relations between our two great nations. God alone knows what they'll be making of it at the Foreign Office.' The old soldier gazed ruefully at us, then a twinkle appeared in his eyes. 'Still, it was a damn good show, nevertheless.'

'But where is Milan?' I said. 'He must take much of the blame or credit for last night. And I for one would very much like to know how he managed to nearly destroy the clinic?'

Mycroft Holmes chuckled. 'Apparently he

was carrying two glass phials containing a mixture of gunpowder, magnesium and phosphorus.'

'A remarkably efficacious mixture of chemicals,' remarked Sherlock Holmes.

'Apparently the mixture is a well-known weapon in the Slav armoury and it has been used to great effect in their continuing war with the Turks,' replied Mycroft.

'It is to that conflict that Milan is now keen to return,' said General Wilton.

'But is the Turkish presence in the area now all but terminated?' I objected.

The general laughed. 'There still remains the question of the Austro-Hungarian annexation of Bosnia-Herzagovina to be resolved. The matter continues to trouble and exercise the minds of Milan and others.'

'And therein lies one of the reasons why I must soon abstract myself from your estimable company, my friends,' said Mycroft. 'The international conference was convened to discuss this matter, among others, and it should not be delayed lest the consequences we so desire to avoid may come to pass.'

'When do you depart, brother?' asked Holmes.

'In the morning, Sherlock. So we have the day together ... let me see, now.' Mycroft stroked his chin thoughtfully for a moment. 'We shall lunch at the *Ristorante la Scala,* close to *La Plazza de Spagna* and then on to the *La casa Del'Opra* where Caruso and Melba are performing *La Boheme.* How does that attract you, my dear fellow?'

Sherlock Holmes smiled. 'It attracts me very well, Mycroft,' he said.

It was late afternoon. Holmes and Mycroft had departed for the opera and as a consequence I found myself at something of a loose end wandering aimlessly in the embassy gardens. It was there that General Wilton sought me out. 'John, my dear fellow. There you are. Will you take tea with me?'

'I should be delighted,' I cried, glad to be able to lift the cloak of boredom that had enveloped me.

He placed his arm around my shoulder and propelled me in the direction of his study. 'It has been a very long while since we have had the opportunity to talk as we did in the old days! Perhaps we may reminisce on our Afghanistan adventures, and after you must tell me something of your long association with Sherlock Holmes.'

Over tea the conversation moved from the tribulations of the newly commissioned officer, through the rugged landscape and harsh climate of Afghanistan to the nature of that country's extraordinary people.

After a while, all talk of the past became exhausted and the conversation turned to the matter of life with Sherlock Holmes and why we had journeyed to Italy. It was only then, whilst going over the matter once more, I realized for the first time, the significance of the arrival of the *Pride of Thanet* and the missing Hunter Andrews.

'Jimmy!' I said urgently. 'Do you suppose that the ship is still impounded in Naples? Or has she been released by the authorities?'

The general laughed. 'Mr Holmes asked me precisely the same question earlier this morning. As a consequence I have asked the carabinieri to transport her master to Rome, so I may question him further.' He took out his watch. 'Let me see. It is just after five… Our man, therefore, should be with us in about three more hours… Time enough, I fancy, for us to finish our tea and enjoy a quiet pipe together.'

Quite as usual, Sherlock Holmes had anticipated the appropriate course of action and had quietly arranged matters accordingly. Although Mycroft had been uppermost in his mind, Holmes had clearly not forgotten the plight of Hunter Andrews, or indeed the grief of his devoted wife.

General Wilton, however, was more intent on discovering something about my life with Holmes.

'John, you know, I have often thought when reading about your adventures together that you have somewhat under-played your part in solving the many problems set before you?'

I waved my hands in a gesture of self-depreciation. 'Thank you, Jimmy. I must tell you, however, I have played only a peripheral part in the cases.'

'Surely, John, there must have been some occasions upon which Holmes had relied upon your advice?'

'I have sometimes been able to advise him on matters medical. Indeed, it is in this area Holmes has regularly deferred to me. It was when we set out upon this very adventure, I took into my care a man who has done us a particularly valuable service.' I laughed at the ruse Holmes and myself had so success-fully played. 'For it is he who is presently residing at the Pargetter Clinic under the name of Sherlock Holmes... Or at least, I suppose he remains so?'

Wilton laughed as well. 'Your subterfuge has remained undiscovered, John. Although

I expect that my report to the Foreign Office of the safe return of Mycroft Holmes at the hands of his brother will undoubtedly percolate into the public arena.'

'Hmm,' I mused. 'Then perhaps we should send a telegram to the clinic warning them of immediate discovery.'

'I'm sorry, old man,' said the general, 'but Mr Holmes has anticipated you again. He has sent a message of warning this very morning.'

I sighed. Once again, like a second-rate pugilist, I had been beaten to the punch by a superior opponent. Any flush of self-importance I had briefly felt whilst producing my meagre catalogue of accomplishment had been cleanly swept away. 'Good old Holmes,' I said through gritted teeth.

A little before seven, Holmes and Mycroft returned. It was plain to see that the hours they had spent together had been quite special.

'Watson, my dear fellow. We have returned from a most enjoyable day. Royally have we wined and dined; and the music of the opera still plays in our ears.'

Mycroft took his brother's hand and shook it warmly. 'Sherlock, my dear. I am away to my bed, for I have an early start in the morning. I do not suppose that we will meet again for some time. So I bid you farewell, brother ... and thank you!'

Holmes clasped his brother's hand between his own and gazed tenderly at him. 'Goodbye, Mycroft. It will not be so long before we meet again.'

Mycroft turned away and walked to the door. Then, for a moment he half turned and looked at me with those fierce intelligent eyes. 'Goodbye, Watson. Thank you also. You are a brave man and it is no wonder Sherlock thinks so dearly of you.'

He turned away once more, opened the door and he was gone. The representatives of the great powers would be his next companions. Perhaps one day I would be fortunate enough to enjoy his company again. It was my sincerest wish so to do.

Holmes slapped me on the back and propelled me in the direction of the dining room. 'Come along, old fellow. We have much to do this night. The master of the *Pride of Thanet* is expected quite soon. We must question him closely about the fate of Hunter Andrews and unless I am very much mistaken, Watson, it is a task that will be best accomplished on a full stomach.

After a thoroughly pleasant meal, General Wilton joined Holmes and me for coffee and cigars. Wilton handed Holmes a file. 'Ah,' said Holmes as he perused the contents. 'Mr Stanley Jefferson, Master of the *Pride of Thanet*. Let me see... Our man has been a mariner for nearly thirty years and he has held a master's ticket for the last seven of those years... Hmm... This is interesting, Watson. His speciality is coasting, with trips to France, Portugal and Italy... His employers are Baker and Musgrove of Dartford. Their trade is in wines and other comestibles... Ah. It seems that friend Jefferson has been sailing close to the wind for some little time. Apparently the port authorities have long suspected him of smuggling, but have yet to uncover any incriminating evidence against him... Well now, I expect we shall be able to assist the authorities with more than enough evidence for their needs now.'

He handed the file to me and I quickly read through it. 'Do you suppose that Mr Jefferson is aware of the fate of Hunter Andrews?' I queried.

'I believe it unlikely, Watson. For as long as he received payment for his cargo, I expect him to know little and care less.'

'Then, what are we to do?'

Holmes looked darkly at me. 'It is quite simple, Doctor. We shall put the fear of God into him.'

A short time later, Mr Stanley Jefferson was shown into the room. He was a tall, bearded man of about fifty. His black hair was grizzled and shot through with grey. His attire was of the usual seaman's type with one exception. His belt was decorated with a gold buckle of the most intricate and singular design. Holmes, I could see, was immediately interested.

The room had been carefully arranged by Sherlock Holmes to impose the greatest possible impression on the seaman. The desk behind which we were seated had been placed at the end of the room farthest from the door, so our visitor had to traverse its entire length, before meeting us.

Behind the desk, Holmes sat on a huge, carved mahogany chair. The seaman was placed, however, on a low stool, which left him virtually peering over the desktop at his interlocutor.

For quite some time Holmes and Wilson simply ignored our visitor and busied themselves with re-reading his file. For myself I took up a position close to the fire, casually leaning on the mantel smoking my pipe and gazing serenely at the seaman.

Sherlock Holmes closed the file and glanced at our visitor. 'Mr Jefferson, you have been brought here to answer for your activities concerning the kidnapping and removal of Mr Hunter Andrews, the attempted murder of Mr Tom Hockney and two others. Also collusion with agents of a foreign power, which, I may add, may lead to further charges of high treason. What do you have to say, sir?'

The sailor glared at Holmes. 'Who are you and what is my business to you?'

Holmes smiled serenely. 'It is right you should know who your accusers are. The gentleman to my right is His Majesty's Ambassador to Italy, General Wilton. The gentleman by the fire is Doctor John Watson and I am Sherlock Holmes.'

The seaman visibly stiffened in his seat. 'Sherlock Holmes?' Jefferson looked uncomfortably at each of us in turn. 'You are not the police. You have nothing on me,' he said defiantly.

'That is where you are wrong, sir. Tom Hockney is alive and well and will testify against you.'

'Hockney alive?'

'Quite so. If you wish it, I shall furnish you with proof positive.' Holmes transfixed the seaman with a piercing look. 'Be assured, Mr Jefferson,' Holmes said darkly. 'I will crush you. Squash you like a fly and give it no more consideration. Believe me, sir, if I can see you hang, I will.'

The sailor began to literally shiver in his seat. If the harsh and icy winds of the Arctic had blown across the room, he would have hardly looked less chilled. 'Very well, Mr Holmes,' he said quietly. 'What do you wish to know?'

Sherlock Holmes glanced in my direction. There was the merest twinkle of amusement in his eye. 'Excellent, Mr Jefferson. We progress. You will firstly tell me about the kidnapping of Mr Hunter Andrews and his fate at the hands of his captors, Wilson and Turner.'

'Well firstly, sir. Are you aware that the men you know as Wilson and Turner are in reality Russian *émigrés?*'

Holmes nodded his assent. 'I do; I do not, however, know their actual names.'

'Then I may be able to help you there, Mr Holmes. Their real names are Michael Shukin and Felix Malinkov. They are refugees from the Tsar's secret police. Malinkov once told me they were active members of an anti-royalist plot to remove the Tsar earlier this century.'

'Do you mean the so-called 1905 Revolution?' I put in.

'I'm sorry, sir, I don't know about that. All I can recall is the name of one of the leading lights. His name was Ulyanov. You know I met him once in early 1907. A cold, intense man, but as he spoke so little English, it would have been difficult to get to know him, I suppose.'

'Hmm...' said Holmes. 'This Ulyanov. Do you happen to recall his appearance?'

'Oh yes, sir. I'll never forget that. He was a bearded man of middle size with a high domed forehead, like an egg his head was, like an egg.'

Holmes and General Wilton exchanged glances. 'Very good, Mr Jefferson,' said Holmes. 'Now perhaps you will explain how you came to be in the company of these people.'

Jefferson cleared his throat nervously. 'Well, Mr Holmes, your earlier remarks have made it clear you are quite aware of my long association with the Russians. So I must tell you that my political views led me to them. For years I have felt that the present system has to be overthrown so that the people can have their fair share of the country's riches...'

Holmes glared at the seaman. 'The facts, Mr Jefferson, if you please.'

'Sorry, Mr Holmes. It was about the time I met Mr Ulyanov, when I was approached by Shukin and Malinkov who, knowing I was sailing for Marseilles, asked me if I would take a package for them. In return they paid me with bottles of vodka. Well, most seamen don't much care for white spirits, so I traded them in at the local pubs, two bottles of vodka for one of rum.' A ghost of a smile passed across the face of the sailor. 'My crew got drunk quite a lot on the fruits of our trade.'

Holmes leaned back in his chair and place his fingertips together. 'Now, sir. Tell me about Mr Andrews.'

Jefferson began to look uncomfortable once more. 'It must have been three weeks ago when Shukin came to me at my lodgings. He said that this time he had a live cargo for me. I thought for a minute he meant an animal of some sort, but he quickly put me straight. He said he had a man, who desperately wanted to get out of the country and back to his home in Italy. Well, sir, it was a bit of a tall order, like. The hands all know what was going on, and a few drinks bought their silence. But I wasn't too sure that they could be relied upon to keep their traps shut. Well, Shukin said that there wouldn't be no problem, they'd bring the man on board a few hours before we sailed, when the crew was still ashore, like. Then they'd settle him down below and when we'd been at sea a bit, I could let him loose and no harm done.'

'Things, however, did not quite go to plan?' said Holmes.

'No, sir, they did not. Firstly, when Shukin and Malinkov brought the man on board, it looked all wrong. He was in a terrible mess, his face was bruised and his hair was flying all over the place, like it hadn't seen a comb for days. He was strangely dressed in a long brown coat several sizes too big for him. Far from him being eager to get on board, they seemed to be dragging him along. Then, as they took him down below, he managed to struggle free and made as if to escape. All the while he was shouting for someone to help him.

'Then Shukov hit him and he crumpled to the deck. Well, sir, it seemed to me that this was as clear a case of kidnapping as one could wish to see. So I asked Shukin what he thought he was playing at. Smuggling was one thing, but this was quite another.

'Well, Mr Holmes. In answer to my question Shukin pulled out a large pistol from his coat and pointed it at my guts. He told me in low tones that my ship would sail on time for the appointed destination and like it or not the man would be our passenger.

'Then Malinkov gave a shout. There was somebody else on the ship. Someone had come back on board. Quickly, I ran back on deck. It was Tom Hockney. Why had he come back? I had no idea. It was clear that he had seen and heard all that had happened, for he took off like a startled rabbit. Shukin shouted something in Russian to Malinkov, who immediately followed Hockney. I was forced back down below by Shukin and we waited for Malinkov's return.

'Well, he didn't come back for several hours. In fact we were about to sail when at last he turned up again. He had missed Hockney in the town, but he made it quite clear he would not be bothering us again. Although he had escaped on the London train, Malinkov had sent messages to his associates in the city that Hockney should be waylaid and dealt with. Shukin ordered me to sail at once. He would stay aboard to watch over his prisoner. Malinkov, he ordered to stay behind to ensure that the business in hand was satisfactorily completed. So we sailed on the early tide, bound, as you know, Mr Holmes, for Naples.'

For the first time since the commencement of the interview, the grizzled sea captain relaxed slightly. But Holmes had not completed his interrogation. 'Thank you, Mr Jefferson. We now have almost all we need to complete the jigsaw. Perhaps you would be kind enough to inform us precisely how you managed to rid yourself of your unwelcome passenger.'

'It was early in the morning when we sighted the Italian coast. We were, I suppose, some two hours from port when Shukin ordered me to make ready with one of the boats. It was his intention to row ashore with Mr Andrews.'

'I imagine you have no idea to where he intended taking his captive?' Holmes asked.

'No, sir, I have no idea.'

Holmes stood up. 'Thank you, Mr Jefferson. I believe I have heard all I need to know.' He turned to General Wilton.

'Indeed, Mr Holmes,' said the general. 'I have set aside a room for Mr Jefferson where he can await further interviews.'

Jefferson looked flustered. 'But my ship, Mr Holmes. I have to be back aboard by tomorrow. We sail for Ramsgate with a cargo of perishables. My employers will be after my blood if I don't get the cargo back on time.'

Holmes transfixed his man with a gimlet stare. 'It is a pity, sir, that you did not concern yourself with the dangers in which your activities were placing you when you commenced smuggling.'

General Wilton gestured to Captain Jefferson that the interview was over. The seaman stood up. It seemed as if he had become considerably shrunken. He had almost reached the door when he stopped and turned back. He produced from an inside pocket a crumpled note and held it out to Sherlock Holmes.

'Perhaps you would like to see this, sir. I'm not too sure if it's of any significance, but I saw Shukin drop it as he departed with Mr Andrews.'

Holmes took the proffered note and scanned it briefly. He held it out for my inspection.

'Here, Watson. What do you make of this?'

I took the note and examined it carefully. At first sight it looked as if the page had been covered with a jumble of alien letters.

Then it occurred to me where I had previously seen something similar. 'Surely, Holmes, this is the same writing that we observed on the coin you discovered on the back step of the Andrews house?'

Holmes laughed. 'Excellent, my boy. You are exactly right, it is Russian.' He took back the note and turned to the seaman. 'Thank you, Mr Jefferson. Someone will no doubt be speaking with you again very soon... Come, Watson, let us seek out Milan for a translation.'

It was much later that evening when Holmes and I sat quietly together before a roaring fire. For the first time in what seemed to be many days we were enjoying a quiet pipe and each other's exclusive company. Holmes took out the note that Jefferson had earlier given him.

The author of the note, realizing that he was writing in a language that few Westerners could read or understand, had made little attempt to disguise his instructions. The wording, however, was still cryptic. It read:

S and M
You will convey our volunteer into the hands of Mr R in Petersburg. Your passage

through the region has been smoothed. Mischa and the Prince are on hand to assist you if any problems arise. You will contact me in R for further instructions when your task is completed.

Good luck

VIU

Holmes glanced at me with raised eyebrows. 'Well, Doctor. Now we have the translation, what do you make of it?'

Again I looked at the note. Holmes, of course, was testing me.

'Well, now,' I said. 'S and M are without doubt Shukin and Malinkov. The volunteer is a euphemism for Mr Andrews. The others mentioned in the note are clearly allies of our author. Whom I might add is presently staying with a friend whose initial is R. What do you think of that?'

'My dear fellow,' said Holmes laughing. 'You excel yourself in stating the obvious.' He took back the paper and looked at it for a few moments. 'Now, let us begin with the contents. You are, of course, quite right in what you have observed, except I believe for the fact that the author of the note is staying in a town rather than with friends.'

'Hmm,' I mused. 'You may be right,

Holmes. It does not place us much farther forward. There must be dozens, if not hundreds, of towns where the initial letter is "R".'

'Well, let us see about that. The writer of this interesting epistle asks Shukin and Malinkov to inform him as soon as their task has been completed. It seems to me that the town in question has to be not too distant from St Petersburg.'

I looked quizzically at Holmes. 'I do not see quite how you have come to that conclusion.'

'Consider this, Doctor. If you had master-minded the kidnapping and transportation of a man with specialist knowledge in order to perform a specific, if as yet unknown, task, would you not ensure yourself of the closest possible residence to the scene of the crime, if not actually in the vicinity itself?'

'Indeed, I would wish to be as close to the centre of activities as possible and to be able to quickly instruct my minions on their further activities. I could not leave myself in a position in which I was unable to act in accordance with events.'

'There you are, my boy,' said Holmes.

'However,' I said thoughtfully. 'I cannot bring to mind any town in Russia, perhaps with the exception of Rostov, which would prove to be suitable for my needs.'

'Ah yes,' said Holmes casually. 'The town we are seeking is not in Russia. It is Riga, in the Baltic States.'

'Oh.'

'Any communication would have you in St Petersburg within four days.' A sudden smile danced across his face. 'A small advantage, nevertheless.'

Clearly this cryptic remark indicated that Holmes had some deep matter on his mind. Quite as usual he was keeping it to himself. I decided, therefore, to raise the matter of the identity of the note's author. 'Holmes?'

'Yes, old fellow?'

'Have you any idea who the mysterious VIU is?'

Holmes looked sharply at me. 'Have you, Doctor?'

'Indeed. I believe him to be the Ulyanov, Jefferson mentioned earlier.'

'My dear fellow...'

'One word, furthermore, I believe him to be of some international importance. Probably he was prominent in the 1905 Revolution in Russia. It further occurs to me, that is why he is presently domiciled in Russia's Baltic States. He is exiled from Russia.'

Holmes laughed and clapped his hands. 'Exactly right. Our man is most certainly Ulyanov.'

'I know I must seem frightfully ignorant, Holmes,' I said tentatively. 'But who exactly is he?'

'He is Vladimir Illych Ulyanov. Depending on your view, he is either a desperate criminal, bent on the destruction of the legitimate establishment, or he is a virtuous patriot, fighting against tyranny and oppression. Either way, he is an intelligent and gifted man, who entirely believes in the rightness of his cause and will brook no interference or avoid any obstacle placed in his path. It is my opinion, Watson, one day, the whole world will come to know his name.'

I sat back in my chair, more than a little pleased with my flash of insight. But I perceived it would do little to further our cause; that of discovering the whereabouts of Hunter Andrews and thereby rescuing him from his captors. Indeed, I could see little merit in pursuing a matter so abstruse and distant. 'This Ulyanov. What does he have in mind for Mr Andrews?' I said gloomily.

'I have presently three theories in my mind, Watson. Without data, however, I cannot say.'

'Then where is Andrews now?'

'Again, without data, Watson...'

'Have you no idea?'

Holmes sighed. 'I have ideas in abundance; and they all lead to one conclusion. In this matter I will have to rely on my intuition and follow where it leads me.'

I looked doubtfully at Holmes. 'And to where does your intuition lead you, Holmes?'

'It leads me to St Petersburg, Watson. It is to there we must go. Then perhaps once in the city of Peter the Great we may discover exactly what lies at the heart of this mystery. Why does an exiled Russian revolutionary have his minions kidnap an anonymous if gifted Englishman and have him secretly transported to Russia? What is the motive? These are deep matters, Watson, and quite a three-pipe problem.' Holmes looked keenly at me and sighed. 'We have no choice; we must follow our Russian friends to St Petersburg for without doubt it is there we shall discover the answers to our questions.'

EIGHT

As the hour of departure was almost at hand, Sherlock Holmes and I had been invited to take coffee with General Wilton in his private sitting room. The general was presently at his desk, but had promised to join us as soon as possible.

In the meantime, Holmes carefully inspected the small wad of currency notes which the Embassy had provided, to be used in each of the countries through which we were to travel. He then tucked away the notes into the secret pocket in his jacket.

He looked at me quizzically. 'How are you feeling about our journey, Watson?'

'A little sad to be leaving under such a cloud and somewhat nervous about what lies before us,' I said, 'but it is also clear to me that Hunter Andrews must be found; and if this is the only avenue open to us, then it has to be the one down which we must travel.'

'Well said, old fellow!' cried Holmes, jumping up and slapping my shoulder. 'If there was another method, be assured I would have employed it.'

I looked through the open French windows and into the gardens beyond, and espied the figures of General Wilton and Milan walking slowly together in the warm morning sunlight, deep in conversation.

'I sincerely hope that the general will be able to persuade Milan to accompany us, for I simply cannot think of any better fellow in a tight corner,' I said, with much feeling.

Holmes nodded, 'Indeed. It is fortunate for us that Milan has also been served with a notice of eviction, so to speak, as his familiarity with the language and the Cyrillic alphabet of Montenegro and Serbia would serve us well.'

The conversation between the General and the Serb seemed to be over, for they quickly made their way up the steps from the garden into the study.

'Ah, coffee,' said Wilton, 'Good morning, John, Mr Holmes, I trust you gentleman slept well?'

'As well as any man who is about to take a step into the unknown, thank you, Jimmy,' I replied.

The general picked up the silver coffee pot and poured out a quantity of the steaming aromatic liquid into four china cups.

'You will be glad to hear, gentlemen, that Milan has agreed to accompany you to the Romanian border.'

Milan took the coffee offered to him by Wilton and sat down at the table beside Holmes.

'Thank you, Milan,' said Holmes.

'I am sorry that I cannot go with you all the way to Russia, gentlemen,' said Milan, 'but there are matters of great importance to be attended to in my own country. I hope you will understand.'

Much relieved that we would have an interpreter to assist our passage through at least some of the strange lands which lay before us, I for one now enjoyed my coffee more than I might have otherwise.

Very early in the planning of our trek, Holmes had insisted that it was essential for us to travel lightly, carrying with us only the barest of essentials.

'Watson,' he told me, 'we must take with us not the things we think we might need; we must rather take only those things we simply cannot do without.'

I looked rather longingly at my unfortunately too large a pile of *essentials* and sighed. 'If you think so, Holmes...' I muttered weakly.

In the end we settled on a large rucksack each and packed into it as many of the items we felt that were necessary. I only hoped that some way into our journey I would not have need of some of those items I had discarded. Fortunately, General Wilton had promised to take care of our property and ensure its safe return to England, where we could collect it at our eventual leisure from the Foreign Office.

When our final goodbyes had been said, Holmes, Milan and myself were taken by carriage to the station and the train which would eventually take us to our final Italian destination of Brindisi. The train was due to depart at eleven a.m., but Italian railways being notorious for their inability to maintain an efficient service did not disappoint us, for the train had been cancelled.

On this particular occasion, however, adverse weather conditions further south had led to delays and the train destined for Rome had been sent back to Brindisi. As one of the staff tackled by Milan explained, this was a *'ghost train'*, that is, one which leaves the point of departure but never arrives at its destination.

Holmes and Milan perused the bulletin

board and discussed the promulgated time of the next departure.

'Well now,' said Holmes. 'It would appear that unless the missing train suddenly makes an appearance, the next departure will be a stopping train, and always assuming that we can pass whatever weather conditions are presently affecting the line, we shall not reach our destination much before our expected sailing time.'

'Will there be a problem?' I asked him.

'No,' he replied, 'but the general should be warned that there may be a delay.' He took out his notebook and perused some notes I had seen him making earlier. 'It is a Greek vessel, the *Zouganelis*; we are supposed to be sailing for Montenegro on the tide at one a.m., but he should be informed never-theless.'

Tea being a beverage virtually unheard of in Italy caused me to remark that if the wait for the next train was to be a protracted one, then would it not be a capital idea if we adjourned somewhere for a cup of coffee. And so it was a little later we found ourselves in a cosy little café drinking from tiny cups and nibbling on a number of small but very sweet *biscotti*.

Becoming rather bored with the seemingly

endless conversation between Holmes and Milan on the peoples and customs of the Balkans, Milan's own region, I gazed aimlessly out of the window at the affairs of the people in the *piazza*. It was a busy area with dozens of carts, carriages and the occasional motor vehicle festooning the area; townspeople in their hundreds were milling about, their faces set firmly in the pursuit of their own agendas, all coming together and resembling a giant ants' nest that had been carelessly stirred up by an unsuspecting boot.

It was as I was contemplating whether I should order another cup of coffee that my attention was drawn to a swiftly moving carriage driven in and out of the perfect scrum of other vehicles in the *piazza* by a driver showing remarkable skills of horsemanship. As the carriage drew to a shuddering halt before the station entrance, I saw a tall figure in white jump down from the step and run like the wind into the concourse; then, after him, stepped down a figure I recognized instantly.

'My word, it's Jimmy,' I said, nudging Holmes, who was by now deeply immersed in a map of the Balkans. 'Surely he cannot be looking for us?'

Holmes folded up the map and tucked it

securely away in the same secret pocket in which he was hiding the money, and looked calmly in the direction of the swiftly disappearing General Wilton. He stood up and indicated that we should follow him.

'My instincts tell me that something has happened,' said Milan, as he stopped to pick up the rucksacks. 'Senior officials do not go about at breakneck speed without good cause.'

We crossed the busy *piazza*, picking our way carefully through the traffic. As we came abreast with the carriage I looked in to see if it contained a face I might recognize, but there remained only the driver, a stranger to my eyes who merely returned my gaze with an unfriendly stare. Then, as we turned into the station entrance, the uniformed man I had just observed running into the station almost collided with me. It was Captain Alfonso Cattini.

'*Scusa, signor,*' he said, clearly not recognizing me in his haste.

'Captain Cattini,' I said, 'it is I, Doctor Watson. What excites you so?'

'Oh, Doctor, Thank heaven,' he said, his countenance turning in a twinkling from troubled to relieved. 'And Mr Holmes. Then you did not take your train after all?'

Holmes gave a little smile. 'No Captain. Apparently adverse conditions somewhere down the line caused the train to be cancelled.'

'Then for one we may be thankful for the Italian railway system,' said Cattini. 'The Ambassador was fearful that the news he has for you would go unreported until it was too late.'

'News? What news?' said Holmes sharply.

The captain looked somewhat abashed and shook his head. 'It is not my place, Mr Holmes, the Ambassador must tell you himself.' His face relaxed into a smile and he lowered his voice and continued in a rather conspiratorial fashion. 'All I can say is that he may have some very good news for you.'

This was most mystifying. Sherlock Holmes and I looked at each other and frowned. Then, as if by magic, we both burst out with the same two words: 'Hunter Andrews!'

'If it is Andrews, Holmes, has he escaped from his captors?'

'Possibly, Watson, possibly. But I see General Wilton bearing down upon us, so we shall have to wait no longer. General...'

'Mr Holmes, John. Thank goodness. I bring news of your friend, Mr Andrews.' Holmes and I exchanged glances and nodded. 'New information sent by one of Captain Cattini's colleagues in Benevento convinces me that he and two others, presumably the Russians you are trailing, have taken up residence in a small hotel, owned and run by another Russian *émigré* called Ignatiev. I might add, they are there because of a landslip caused by a spell of inclement weather having blocked the line. What do you think of that, Mr Holmes?'

If, upon reception of this information, the general was expecting praise and congratulations, he was to be sadly disappointed. Holmes, at the best of times, never was the fellow to waste or time of such trivia as he saw it, he merely demanded of the Ambassador that some form of transportation be provided so that the matter could be brought to a swift and final conclusion.

'The next train, if it appears, is not due for an hour. The journey will take four hours and forty minutes. Is there another method by which we might get to Benevento more quickly?'

The general shook his head. 'I cannot see how, Mr Holmes. Rail, even in this country, is so much quicker than road. Even if you were to leave now, the train would arrive before our carriage.'

'A motor car. Have you no motor car, General?' said Holmes severely. 'Is it not beyond the wit of His Majesty's Ambassador to obtain one in an emergency? Can the police do nothing?'

General Wilton said nothing to Holmes, but a sharp intake of breath clearly revealed his feelings. He turned to the policeman and they engaged in a brief conversation. I looked at Holmes and saw his face to be a perfect mask of concentrated determination, and then, just for the briefest of moments, the mask slipped and the corner of one eye crinkled into what I could have sworn to be the merest hint of a wink, then his face returned to its original visage.

'Mr Holmes,' said Wilton, turning back to face him once more, 'I believe that the captain has a solution to this matter. He is indeed able to lay his hands on a motor vehicle. It is the one usually reserved for the use of one of his superior officers, but he is presently in Turin, so it is now standing idle. It is therefore at your disposal.'

Sherlock Holmes nodded. 'Thank you, General. Thank you, Captain. How long will you need to make the necessary arrangements?'

Captain Cattini took out his watch and looked at it. I could see that he was doing a quick mental calculation.

'It could be ready for you in thirty minutes.'

Holmes nodded and rubbed his hands together briskly. 'Excellent. Then we shall retire to the café from whence we have just come and wait there for your return. Coffee, Watson?'

It was rather less than thirty minutes later when Holmes and I found ourselves racing through the busy streets of Rome in the direction of Benevento some one hundred miles to the south-east of the capital. Our transport, a large black vehicle, furnished as comfortably as one would suppose it to be as the regular transporter of a very senior policeman. The driver apart, our sole companion was Captain Cattini, for, realizing that he would be superfluous to requirements, Milan had returned to the Embassy with General Wilton to await the outcome and our return.

As the vehicle sped along, the captain explained how news of the Russian kidnappers had come to his notice.

'It was early last evening when a report of

a landslip on the line between Avellino and Benevento was delivered to my office. Then, just afterwards, the town's senior police officer telephoned to ask if I could send some men to assist with the transferring of passengers to local hotels for the night, or where appropriate, in sending those who desired, back to Rome.

'Apparently no one was hurt in the incident, except for one fellow who appeared to be somewhat disorientated. The officer thought him to be a foreigner who spoke no Italian. He was in the company of two other men, also foreigners. One was a tall blond fellow and the other was a shorter balding man who fortunately did speak our language. He informed the officer that the wild-looking fellow was a mental incompetent who was being transferred from the Bixio Clinic near Rome to his home in Greece.'

Holmes sat up very straight in his seat. 'The Bixio Clinic?' he said sharply.

Cattini laughed. 'The very same establishment as the one your Serb friend Milan Spasich nearly destroyed a few days ago. As soon as I heard the name Bixio an alarm bell was set off in my head. So I took out the file on your escapade and after reading it carefully I rang back to my officer and asked him to keep a watch on these fellows until further notice. Then I telephoned your Ambassador and put the case to him. The rest, Mr Holmes, you know.'

Holmes nodded. 'Excellent, Captain Cattini. Given the information available, you have come to the exact conclusions I myself would have come to. I congratulate you.'

'Thank you, Mr Holmes,' he said, bowing his head slightly in recognition. 'Praise from one so illustrious as yourself is a reward indeed.'

We had covered scarcely a dozen miles when the sky began to darken and a heavy and persistent rain began to fall and we were quickly in the middle of a violent thunderstorm. Thunder and lightning raged all around and the driver began to complain. Clearly he was unhappy about continuing. Cattini nodded his consent and the car pulled into a quiet roadside layby. It was scarcely any wonder, I mused, that further on a landslip had engulfed the railway line.

The captain felt in his pocket and produced a packet of cigarettes. Holmes, in the meantime, consulted his watch. The delay, although quite necessary, was irksome to him. Nevertheless, and all the while whilst we waited for the rain to abate, his fingers ceaselessly drummed on the car's window-sill; much to my intense irritation, I must say.

Then, at last, the conditions improved and before long we were racing along the Benevento road. Towns and villages slipped by and eventually we rumbled into the outskirts of the town. The road ran over a hump-backed bridge spanning a high and angry-looking river, its waters boiling and bubbling as it swiftly ran along its course. Then, as the car slowed and turned into the road leading down to the railway station. I could see considerable deposits of mud, branches and other debris built up on the roadside. Clearly, in the very recent past, there had been a considerable amount of rain and some flooding hereabouts.

The car pulled up outside the railway station and Cattini jumped out. Holmes and I followed at a more leisurely pace, picking our way carefully through the flood debris, and by the time we had found our way into the foyer the captain had discovered the officer he had arranged to meet. They held the briefest of conversations in Italian, then Cattini introduced us to his colleague.

'Gentlemen, this is Inspector Inzaghi. The Inspector's English is quite good, but speak a little more slowly for his benefit, if you please.'

Inzaghi bowed and soberly shook hands with Holmes and myself. 'Signor Holmes and Doctor Watson. It has been my desire to meet you. If I can help you in any way, please to ask me.'

'Thank you, Inspector,' said Holmes. 'Those foreign nationals you have spoken to Captain Cattini about, can you describe them for me, please?'

'Ah, *si*. Two of the men were Russians. One was a little bald fellow and the other was tall with ... yellow head ... *si?* But the other fellow, he was dark, like gypsy. The little bald Russian, he say, fellow Greek and they are taking him from a clinic near Rome back to his home in Greece when the accident on railway happen. This fellow, he looked wild and like a lost child and my heart feel very sad for him.

'Then the Russian, he asks me if there is any way they can get to Brindisi now. I tell him not for a day maybe two. So he then asks if a hotel can be found and when I tell him about the *Romanov* and how it is run by Russian *émigré* he is very happy to be taken there.

'So I direct one of my men to take them

there, and as far as I know they stay there still.'

'Excellent,' said Holmes. 'You have made sure a policeman is watching the hotel all of the time?'

The inspector nodded vigorously. 'Indeed, Signor Holmes. I have two of my men in attendance.' He chuckled. 'Actually, I have one man sitting in the, how you say ... pub, *si*? He is drinking and watching. It is one command I give him he obeys with joy.'

'Quite so,' said Holmes. 'Now, Captain, how many men can you spare us when we confront these villains?'

Cattini gave the matter a little thought. 'I believe that I can spare you a further three, Mr Holmes.'

'Very good. If they can stand guard outside in the hotel grounds, whilst Doctor Watson and I, and of course yourself, Captain, arrest those fellows, then that will be excellent.'

Quite as usual, Sherlock Holmes with his quiet, cool, authoritative manner was able to take control of the situation and the senior policemen were bent to his will without demur. The motor car was brought round to the station foyer and before long we were travelling along the road and into the district of Benevento where the Hotel Romanov was situated.

As we motored along, the rain began to fall once more, and as we made our way up the leafy hill to the corner where the hotel stood, little rivers of rainwater began to run down the gulleys between the road and the grassy banks to each side.

Acting upon Holmes's instructions, the car was pulled up a hundred yards or so from the hotel. We jumped out and ran quickly up the slope, keeping to the lee of the overhanging trees and avoiding as much of the downpour as possible. Then, just yards from our destination, a policeman brandishing a rifle stepped out from the undergrowth and challenged us.

But, seeing the uniforms of Cattini and Inzaghi, he stood to attention and saluted. After a brief conversation, the policeman turned and led us along a heavily overhung pathway. Then, at last, we stood before our object of desire, the Hotel Romanov.

We were preparing our plan of action in the shelter of a large barn situated in the hotel grounds when Holmes turned to me. 'Watson, you have your service revolver with you? Very good. Then I have a little task for you.'

'You know me, Holmes. I am ready for anything.'

He smiled briefly, then looking up at the building he addressed the inspector. 'Inzaghi, do you know in which room our friends are to be found?'

The policeman swiftly conversed with his colleague, then he pointed to a window on the first floor. 'As much as I know, all men are staying in the same room, so it will be simple to catch them like the fish in the same net, no?'

Holmes grunted but made no comment, on more than one occasion we had discovered that finding our villains was one thing, but rounding them up successfully could be quite another! As the old proverb says, *There's many a slip 'twixt the cup and the lip*. Notwithstanding, whilst the inspector and his men took up their positions in the rain, Holmes, Cattini and I entered the hotel.

It was dingy inside, but a cheery enough fire was burning in the grate and all-enveloping warm fug, strong with the smell of baking, cheeses and furniture polish, permeated the atmosphere.

There was but one other patron in the bar. This fellow had to be the police officer

226

deployed by Inzaghi, for once our entrance he stood up and made signal to the inspector that he recognized who we were.

A short bearded man in shirtsleeves, wearing a long white apron and a broad smile, appeared from a doorway towards the rear of the lounge; his hands were all floury. *'Bonjourno, signori.* Pardon the delay, but I am making bread for tonight's supper.' Then, as he recognized the uniform of the carabinieri, his face fell. *'Il Capitano,* I sincerely hope that nothing is amiss?'

Briefly, the captain explained who we were and the reason for our business. The proprietor, for it was he, looked abashed. 'I am sorry, *Capitano,* but I honestly believed my fellow Russians were taking a sick friend home for treatment.'

By now, Holmes was becoming impatient, to employ his own words, now that the game was afoot there was no time to waste. 'We need the key to their room. Instruct your man to keep a sharp eye on this fellow. Honest patron or no, he may still be inclined to warn his compatriots.'

The captain nodded and commanded the policeman to watch the Russian. Then, taking the key in one hand and his pistol in the other, Holmes led Cattini and myself up the dingy wooden stairs to the first floor and the lair of our enemies.

For a few seconds Holmes held us up at the top of the stairs. 'Now, gentlemen, if you will follow my instructions to the letter we may avoid the need for any violence, but if the life of Hunter Andrews seems to be in any danger, shoot his kidnappers without mercy.'

Captain Cattini looked at Holmes with a mixture of admiration and surprise. 'Excellent, Mr Holmes. That is exactly what I would tell my men in similar circumstances. But now, sir, officially this is my responsibility and I insist on going first into the room.'

The two men regarded each other for a moment, then Sherlock Holmes nodded. 'Of course, Captain Cattini. I am a stranger in a strange land and, as you say, this is your responsibility,' He looked darkly at the policeman. 'But remember this, Cattini, we are still dancing to my tune.'

The captain nodded and knocked loudly as the door.

'*Si?*' came the muffled response from within.

'Room service, *signor.*'

'But we have ordered nothing,' came the rejoinder.

'A bottle of wine, with the compliments of Signor Ingnatiev.'

'Oh, very well!'

There came the sound of the key being turned in the lock and the door was opened an inch or two. A shrewd face peered out and, before he could react, Cattini gave the door a sharp kick and literally knocked the little balding Russian to the floor. As the door flew open and hit the wall with a bang, I could see the other inhabitants of the room. One was a tall blond fellow with a moustache whom I instantly recognized as Shukin, the villain who had come to Cliff House full of murderous intent towards Holmes and myself.

Clearly he recognized me too. 'You!' he ejaculated.

I pointed my service revolver squarely at his heart. 'Yes,' I agreed, 'it is I. No, do not attempt to move, for I shall surely shoot you down just as you once shot down Vincent Parker.'

Shrugging his shoulders, Shukin smiled and raised his hands above his head. 'Ah well, Doctor Watson ... and Mr Holmes! You have me cold, no? I will not resist you, for I have no Mr Parker to act as my shield this time!'

A sharp pang of anger swelled in my breast at this callous remark made so casually by the Russian, and this was to prove a stupid error for Shukin was by no means ready to admit defeat and for the briefest of moments, my emotions took over from my concentration, I allowed him the luxury of the chance to react and he reacted by literally throwing himself at my legs and knocking me spinning into the unsuspecting Captain Cattini. As we fell heavily into each other we also sent the table crashing, and its contents were scattered to the four corners of the room.

As I hit the floor, I jarred my elbow, sending a sharp stab of pain running through my forearm, and more seriously, a nervous reaction in my fingers, which resulted in the unintentional firing of my service revolver. The loud bang and the shattering of the window pane caused Cattini to recoil sharply and even Sherlock Holmes to take precautionary avoiding action. Shukin, seizing his chance, with remarkable dexterity, literally rolled himself out of the room and into the corridor beyond.

Holmes hauled me to my feet and shouted at me, 'Did you see in which direction he has exited?'

I shook my head.

'Very well. Go up to the top of the stairs whilst I look downstairs... Hurry, man or he will get away!'

Cattini was by now scrambling to his feet. He looked somewhat dazed by the whole episode and I helped to steady him.

'My apologies, Captain,' I said, 'I allowed my concentration to slip.'

'Well, do as Holmes has instructed,' Cattini said hotly, 'and see that you do not make such a mistake again!'

Angered not only by my own stupidity but also by my companion's reaction to it, I ran out into the deserted corridor and quickly ascended the steps to the top floor, hardly aware of the possible danger I could be dashing headlong into. Then, on the top landing, I saw that the window was wide open and the rain was getting in. Of Shukin, however, there was no sign. As I looked out I could see the bough of a huge tree only a few feet away from the ledge. Had Shukin risked all and, in a frantic effort to escape, jumped from the window into the tree?

Yes, he had, for not more than fifteen feet below there was the figure of the blond Russian sliding down the trunk of the tree. The rain was by now simply pouring, and it splattered onto my head and shoulders, soaking them within seconds.

'Holmes!' I cried. 'Here is your man!'

Moments later, the figures of Sherlock Holmes, Inspector Inzaghi and two police-man were bearing down upon the fleeing Russian. Then the ground beneath his feet gave way and he slipped and fell, his footing lost in the black slurry into which the hillside was rapidly turning. Before he knew what was happening, Shukin found himself at the feet of Holmes and three policemen, with their guns trained upon him.

Back in the hotel room, I found Captain Cattini to be fully in control of the situation. In my absence, he had bound Malinkov, the balding kidnapper, and was sitting on an upright chair regarding the prostrate form of Hunter Andrews on the bed.

I quickly examined Andrews, who had lain totally oblivious to all that had gone on in the room and beyond. Captain Cattini came and peered over my shoulder. 'How is the poor fellow, Doctor Watson?'

'He seems to be in the grip of some powerful narcotic,' I replied. 'Possibly it is laudanum; but he appears otherwise unhurt in any way. I expect that his captors were able to keep him quiet by administering doses at regular intervals.'

Captain Cattini sighed. 'I can feel only contempt for those who have used him so badly. Let us sincerely hope that very soon he will be back home safe in the bosom of his family.'

Sherlock Holmes and I stood in the hotel lounge, brandy and soda in hand, and looking out of the window at the grounds and the woods beyond. It was still raining but somehow the weather conditions mattered not a jot, for at long last Hunter Andrews was safe and well, and our enemies were under lock and key.

With an efficiency I felt to be perfectly unique in a country famed for its official unreliability, Captain Cattini had quickly arranged for transport to take away the two Russians for incarceration and for Andrews to be examined by a police doctor. Ignatiev, the Russian hotelier, would be interviewed later.

'Well now, Doctor,' said Holmes, with the ghost of a smile playing about his lips, 'perhaps we may finally be in a position to declare this case to be closed.'

'Hmm,' I agreed. 'It is a pity, however, that we are still to be thrown out of Italy, for I would very much have liked to see some of her sights before returning home again.'

'Indeed. But perhaps in the future, when our misdeeds are forgotten, we may be made welcome again. Then, my dear fellow, we shall travel as we please.'

I sighed. 'Well, perhaps. But we have to get our affairs in London resolved before all else. You really cannot have the newspapers continuing to brand you as a madman, nor can Tom Hockney be detained at the Pargetter Clinic longer than is absolutely necessary.'

Holmes laid down his glass and sat with his legs crossed in a comfortable armchair. He felt for his pipe and vesta case. 'We also have the small matter of Chief Inspector Lestrade to consider, Watson. Although it is not the first occasion on which he had been made to look foolish, nor do I suppose it to be the last, we are responsible for playing a foul trick on him.'

'Quite so,' I agreed, 'he will be deeply offended.'

Holmes lit his pipe and blew rings of smoke into the air. He smiled. 'Then, my dear fellow, we shall play upon his sense of loyalty and duty to the crown and tell him that, without his albeit unwitting co-operation, none of these good works could have been accomplished.'

It was a little before suppertime when Holmes and I found ourselves once more in the company of General Wilton. We three sat at the well-provisioned table and I, for one, was more than ready to do proper justice to the spread set out before us. The meal proved to be a relaxed and most enjoyable affair, for our little *hiatus* apart, as Jimmy called it, the mission to Rome had proved to be a success. No longer did the prospect of travelling over unknown lands lay before us; only the eager anticipation of returning to London was now stirring in our breasts.

A telephone bell rang in the distance and it was followed by a light tap upon the door. The head and shoulders of an embassy official peered round it and a hand was gestured at General Wilton; the call was for him.

The general retrieved the napkin from his knee, folded it and threw it onto his plate. 'It is always the same. As soon as I imagine that all my problems are behind me, another one arises to vex me.' He stood up and walked over to the door. 'Gentlemen, please take your coffee by the fire. I shall not be more than two or three minutes.'

Holmes and I eased ourselves into the deep leather armchairs either side of the cheerful blaze. We smoked our pipes and, in the manner of the old days, sat there silent and glad to be so in the exclusive company of each other.

Suddenly this atmosphere of calm reflection was rudely shattered by the return of General Wilton. His face was white as chalk and he looked disturbed in the extreme.

'Good heavens, Jimmy! What is the matter?' I cried.

Without stopping to answer, my old army colleague almost ran over the dresser, picked up the decanter and poured himself a stiff brandy. He gulped it down in one go, then more slowly he poured two more glasses and brought them over to Holmes and myself.

'Mr Holmes, John. You will scarcely believe it, but I have just taken a telephone call from Captain Cattini. He has informed me that the Russians you have worked so diligently to capture have managed to escape from the police station at Benevento.'

'How so?' cried Holmes, literally jumping to his feet.

'It seems that the men were put in a cell together, prior to interrogation. Then, after a little while, Malinkov called out to the guard that Shukin was ill. When the fellow looked into the cell, he could see him writhing on the floor with Malinkov crouching over him presumably in an attempt to see what he could do to assist him. Momentarily forgetting that this was a police cell, the guard also knelt down to look at the stricken Russian. Before he knew it, the pair fell upon him, knocked him out and took his gun. Then, with the element of surprise favouring them, Shukin and Malinkov simply disappeared into the growing darkness. A hunt ensued, but the rain, mud and poor light hampered their search and the pair could not be found.'

Holmes bit his lip in frustration. 'This is not good news, General.'

Wilton pulled a face and sighed deeply. 'I have news of an even blacker hue,' he said quietly, his face colouring. 'I also have to report that Hunter Andrews is missing.'

For myself, I was wide-eyed and speechless with surprise and outrage. Sherlock Holmes, however, was not. He merely nodded. 'It follows that they would not have given up their mission so lightly,' he said evenly. 'How was it achieved?'

'It would seem that Mr Andrews was being treated by the police doctor in the same building and he had been left alone to rest. When the Russians broke out they simply snatched him away, for no guard was left on him... Mr Holmes, I do not know quite what to say...'

I looked sympathetically at the general. It was scarcely his fault that this disaster had occurred and I sincerely hoped that Holmes would not be in the mood to shoot the messenger, so to speak. Turning my gaze upon him, high in the expectation of his ire pouring forth, I was frankly surprised to find my companion to be serenity itself.

Holmes laid down his pipe upon the small table and relaxed once more into his seat and flashed a brief smile. 'Well now, Doctor, unless I am wrong we are to pay a visit to St Petersburg after all.' His gaze turned towards General Wilton. 'General, will you please send for Milan. I wish to talk to with him.'

This Large Print Book, for people
who cannot read normal print,
is published under the auspices of

THE ULVERSCROFT FOUNDATION